MARKED TO THE OMEGA

THE LUNA BROTHERS MPREG ROMANCE SERIES

Stay updated with sales and new releases by subscribing to Ashe Moon's personal newsletter! Scan the QR code below with your phone camera!

* * *

If you're looking for something a little more personal you can also join my private Facebook group, **Ashe Moon's Ashetronauts**!

My group is a safe space to chat with me and other readers, and where I also do special exclusive giveaways and announcements. Hope to see you there!

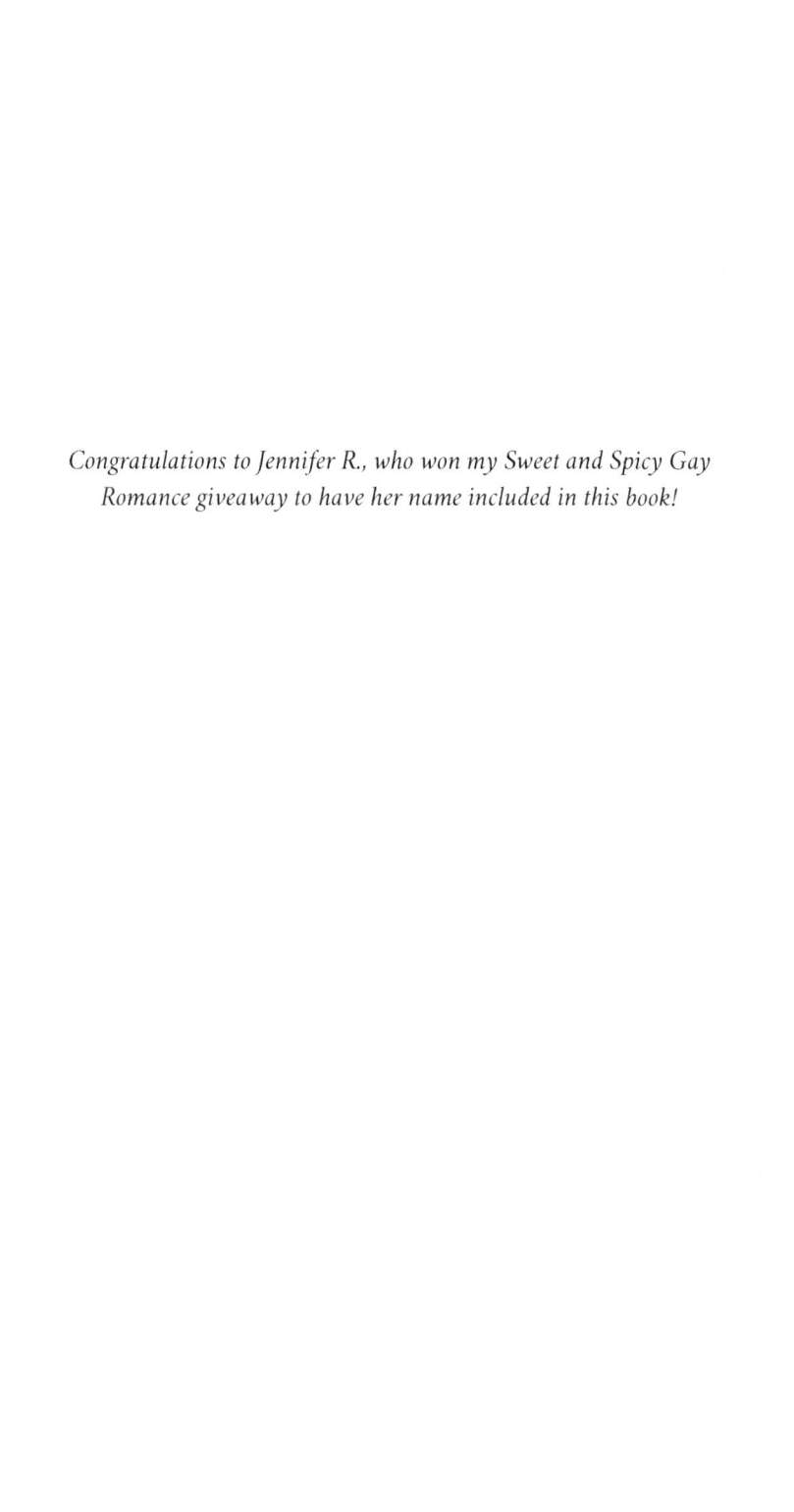

Congratulations to Jennifer R., who won my Sweet and Spicy Gay Romance giveaway to have her name included in this book!

THE LUNA BROTHERS

Loch's Story - Wed to the Omega
Vander's Story - Doctor to the Omega
Arthur's Story - Bound to the Omega

CHRISTOPHE

*S*o much of my early childhood was a blur in my mind, marked by vivid flashes of memory that have lived with me until now, unable to be forgotten. I could still clearly remember the first time I successfully shifted into my wolf form when I was four years old, Mother and Father watched from the side, surrounded by the silhouettes of my relatives. Uncle Edsel was there, as was Grandmother. Arthur, my little brother, was there too. He was just a baby, wrapped up in Mother's arms.

The transformation came naturally. Father had told me what to expect, and I'd already been experiencing the precursors to a full shift for weeks before; my wolf ears suddenly sprouting from the top of my head, one foot randomly turning into a paw, pants ripping due to an unexpected tail, those kinds of things. I stood alone in the middle of a circular clearing in the woods near the Luna Manor, the eyes of my family trained on me. I closed my eyes and concentrated on the wolf that I could feel inside me, straining to be freed. I could feel my bones moving inside my body. They were changing shape, breaking apart, clicking into new places. When I opened my eyes and looked down at my hands, my fingertips were drawing backward into themselves, my nails becoming claws and my skin sprouting dark fur. I was frightened for a moment, but Father had told me not to be scared, so the feeling passed quickly and was replaced by excitement. I was a wolf. I'd completed my first shift and started my journey towards my destiny as the first alpha of the Luna family, leaders of the Crescent Moon Pack.

The memories of the shift ceremony were often tangled up with those of visiting the Teller about a year later, when I was five years old.

I remembered Father's seemingly gigantic hand wrapped around my own as we walked through the candlelit passageway to the Teller's chambers. The sanctum smelled strongly of pine incense, like the smoke from a forest fire, all combined with the metallic tang of the animal blood often used for divination. I was frightened at the idea of how the blood would be used—would I be soaked in it? Have to drink it?

"Christophe Luna," the Teller said, his voice harsh like gravel. He wore a heavy, black velvet cloak with a hood that hid everything about his face except for a long and grizzled snout that protruded from shadow. He was in half-shift form; part wolf, part man. "First son of Basch and Stella Luna. Come forward."

. . .

Father released my hand and took a step back into darkness, leaving me alone. I did my best to be brave, as brave as a five-year-old could be. "Yes," I said, stepping forward into the circle of candlelight.

"Remove your clothing," the Teller said.

I hesitated, uncertain about what to do. I looked over my shoulder at Father, who nodded at me. I slowly stripped out of my clothes and stood naked in the circle, goosebumps spreading across my skin. The Teller stepped slowly into the circle of candlelight, and a dance of light illuminated his eyes beneath the hood. I gasped when I saw them. They were milky white with cataracts—sightless—but I felt that he could see *everything*. He towered over me and circled a bony, clawed hand above my head, palm spread open. In his other hand, he held the skull of some animal draped in golden chains inset with glimmering green and red gems. The skull held incense, and piney smoke billowed out from the eye sockets. I was terrified, and squeezed my eyes shut. My ears pricked up at the sound of the Teller moving around me, his feet shuffling on the stone floor.

The Teller murmured to himself, growling incantations and prayers in a language I couldn't understand. I opened my eyes again. He circled around me, moving like liquid darkness under the shimmer of the candles, and the smoke from the skull drifted close the ground, creating an ethereal haze of tendrils that seemed like they were going to reach up and grab me. He stopped in front of me and dipped a thumb into a depression on the top of the skull. His thumb returned coated and dripping in blood. He pressed his thumb to my forehead and dragged it down until it reached the space between my eyes.

"Yes… Yes, I see," he said. "You will be a loyal wolf of high ideals. You will rise when the occasion calls for protecting what you hold dear. And…" He paused and cocked his head, sniffing at the air. "What is this? There's something… Your leg."

"My leg?"

"The mark on your leg…"

"It's a birthmark," I said, proudly. The mark was a dark coloration on my right inner thigh about the size of my palm, and looked just like a wolf's paw print with one pad missing. "Mother says it's lucky."

"Hmm… This is no ordinary birthmark," the Teller said. He waved the animal skull, and a drape of smoke drifted down through the air. I coughed.

"What do you mean?" Father said.

"This is… rare."

. . .

"What is it?" Father asked impatiently.

"This is the mark of a fated mate," the Teller said to me. "It's a mystical marking, one of the few that still occur. Somewhere in the world there is, or will be, a wolf whose paw print will perfectly match this mark."

"A fated mate?" I asked. I was nervous, uncertain what this meant.

"Yes," the Teller replied in his rasping voice. He intertwined his gnarled fingers in front of him. "A soul mate who you will be drawn to, and fall deeply in love with, and them with you. The ultimate partnership. The ultimate mated pair. Your bond cannot be broken by anything, because it is one created by destiny."

Father sat across from me in the back of the family car during the drive home. He pulled out a crystal bottle from the fridge inset into the car door and poured himself a glass. "There's no such thing as a fated mate mark, Christophe," he told me. "It's nonsense."

"There isn't?" I asked.

"No, Christophe, there isn't. What you have is just a birthmark."

. . .

"But how did he know it was there? He was blind."

"Don't underestimate a wolf's fully developed sense of smell, especially when they can't use their eyes."

"You and Mother don't have marks?"

"Christophe, seeing the Teller is just a ritual we must perform in respect to tradition. What you must learn as the firstborn alpha of our family, Christophe, is that there is no such thing as fate, except for the responsibilities expected of you from your family. Don't relegate your purpose in life to romantic ideas."

"Yes, Father," I answered, and for the next twenty-two years of my life I kept my hope that I would someday find the fated love of my life.

* * *

I strode down the hallway to begin my morning routine of waking up my brothers, one that I'd done nearly my entire life. I stopped in front of my youngest brother Vander's door, and held my knock. Vander was gone. It'd slipped my mind that he'd left home to go up north on a little "journey of self-discovery" after failing to get into the Dawn Academy's renowned Fighting Arts School. It'd always been Vander's dream to become a fighter, so his decision to leave was understandable. I'd be lying if I said I wasn't just a bit jealous. Being an omega gave Vander certain family advantages that

Mother and Father would never allow for the rest of us alpha brothers, especially me. I was the eldest, after all. I had a responsibility to my family to take over as clan leader, and that meant handling many family affairs, including wrangling my younger brothers on my parents' behalf. There'd never been time or the opportunity for adventure in my life.

I passed the door to Loch's old bedroom. My youngest alpha brother was a married man now, and had moved out of the family home about three years ago. Now *that*'d been a surprise. Loch had always been the least disciplined of the family. It was always difficult for the youngest alpha, especially when you're the youngest of three other alphas. I understood Loch's struggle, but never eased off him. I felt like the only way I could fulfil my duties as his older brother was to be as strict with him as Mother and Father would be. In the end, I supposed it worked out. He made his way through the Fighting Arts School with exceptional marks, and the omega he'd initially been wed to through an arrangement between families turned out to be perfect for him.

At twenty-seven, I was still single. The eldest, a graduate of the Dawn Academy's Alpha Leadership College, and by all rights the most eligible bachelor of the Luna brothers. In the back of my mind, I suppose I always believed that I would be the first to find love because of what the Teller had told me about my birthmark, but here I was, without even one single relationship under my belt.

I'd never stopped believing that the mark meant something special, even though I kept my feelings about it completely to myself. I would look at it sometimes and wonder if there really was a person out there with a paw print that matched the dark smudges of skin, like brown ink spilled onto my thigh. It did feel a little ridiculous, believing in something like that, especially as I got older. Maybe Father had been right all along.

I raised my hand to knock on Arthur's door, but he opened it before I could. "Morning," he said, and I moved aside to let him pass. The two of us walked together down to the dining room where we were meant to join Mother and Father for family breakfast.

"You know, Christophe, I don't need you to come knocking on my door every morning. I don't require any wakeup call."

"A force of habit," I said, readjusting the cuffs of my shirt and straightening my jacket. "Now that Vander and Loch are gone, I don't have anyone to boss around. Be kind to me and let me continue to do the one thing I'm good at."

Arthur cracked a smile, and we turned down the hallway lined with tall, painted portraits of our ancestors, the eyes of whom felt as if they were tracking us as we walked. When we were children, my brothers would follow closely behind me every time we had to walk through this hallway, each of them holding on to the other's arm or shirt. The paintings made me feel just as uneasy, but as the eldest brother I had to put on a brave face.

. . .

The Luna family was one of the oldest in Wolfheart, and our clan, the Crescent Moons, was one of the most powerful. Any anxiety I used to have walking through this hallway of my ancestors had long disappeared and been replaced by pride. Each portrait reminded me of the great men and women who had come before me, and who had worked to protect this family's legacy. At the end of hallway on opposite walls were paintings of Mother and Father. Eventually, my portrait would be included here, along with the portrait of my future mate.

If I ever found one.

It wasn't like the chance hadn't ever come up in the past. I'd had relationships, but none of them ever seemed to work out. Whose fault it was, I don't know. Maybe it was mine. Maybe I was holding on to the hope that my fated soul mate was really out there, somewhere.

"Excited for Ian's party?" Arthur asked. Ian was our soon to be four-years-old nephew, Loch's little boy. Mother and Father had arranged for there to be a big celebration for his birthday tonight, and several of the wealthiest and most powerful allied clans had been invited. For Mother and Father, it would be a chance to schmooze with the other family heads, make new connections and re-polish old friendships. For young alphas like Arthur and myself, it meant getting friendly with all the other eligible betas and omegas from other families. Arthur was teasing me. He knew my outward stoicism towards romance was a front. Of course I was excited at the prospect of meeting someone. Meeting *the* someone.

It was difficult being highborn. There were expectations of us to mate with someone who was worthy, which basically meant other highborn or those with some kind of status, and now that I'd graduated from the Academy, it'd been difficult to meet new potential mates. Also, I was so damn busy all the time with my duties—looking out for my brothers, helping my parents, learning the skills I'd need to eventually become clan leader. It was all so overwhelming, and sometimes…

Sometimes I wished I could just escape from it all. Leave it all behind.

"Nowhere near as excited as you," I said. "Try to behave, Arthur. It's Ian's birthday party, not a matchmaking party. Don't make anyone feel uncomfortable. I know how damn forward you can be sometimes."

"I have no idea what you mean," he replied coyly. "I'm friendly."

"You're a flirt."

He shrugged. "And you're a prude. Lighten up, Christophe. You know Mother and Father arranged this thing as an excuse for us to meet some hotties."

"I don't know if I'd put it that way," I said. He was right, but I was trying to be proper. Again, force of habit. Maybe I was a prude, but I felt like I had to be one. There was a lot riding on my shoulders, after all. But I *was* excited. Who knew, maybe something would actually happen tonight? I'd do my duty as host and the eldest, but once the pleasantries were out of the way and everyone was settled, I'd make my rounds just like Arthur.

Well, maybe not *just* like Arthur. I'd be more restrained.

"Good morning, Mother. Father," I said as we entered the dining room. The two of them were already at the table eating their breakfast, staring at their tablets.

"It's going to snow up there," Mother said. "Do you think Vander is alright?"

"He's fine, Stella," Father said. "Good morning, Christophe. Arthur."

"Good morning, boys," said Mother. "Wow. Look at this." She pointed at her tablet. "'Mysterious string of break-ins in the Blackwood District, third clan estate targeted.' They still haven't caught this thief? How frightening. And the Blackwood District is so close to us."

"Do the police have leads?" I asked.

"It doesn't seem like it," she said, scanning the article. "They slip in and out undetected. It says that sometimes they don't even notice anything is missing until weeks later."

"Must not have been stealing anything important, then," Father said, looking back to his tablet.

"Brushing up on the current events, eh, Dad?" Arthur said, clapping Father's shoulder on his way over to the serving table. I followed him. The table was stocked with the usual spread of breakfast items, all prepared by the wait staff of the Luna household. Cereal, freshly baked loaves of bread, cut fruit, plump sausages, thick cut bacon, eggs, grilled tomatoes, baked potatoes tossed with caramelized onions, piping hot soup, and pitchers of milk, coffee and tea. I chose a few of my favorites—I loved the way our chef made the bacon, crispy, but not enough so that it wasn't slightly fatty and juicy. Arthur took a bowl of cereal and some fruit.

Father grunted. "Just like you ought to be. You know the Rose Claw, Crooked Tail, and Golden Forest clans will be here tonight? Along with the Ice River clan, of course. Three of the wealthiest, most well-bred clans in Wolfheart, and all their leading members."

Arthur shrugged. "Just show me to the single ones, and I think I'll be fine."

. . .

"Hounds of Hell," Father said, looking up from his tablet to give Arthur an incredulous glare. "Please try to be dignified, Arthur. These are important people. We don't want to reflect poorly on our clan."

"I'll behave," Arthur said with a little smile. "Though let's not kid ourselves. We all know this party is for more than just celebrating Ian's birthday. He winked at me, and I rolled my eyes, but couldn't restrain a smile. "Christophe and I will be having our fun. Too bad Van's not here."

"Just a second," Mother said, putting down her tablet. "That reminds me. I received an e-mail last night from your uncles in Lupania. Your cousins will be coming to the party."

"Cousin Volk and Lukas?" Arthur said, surprised. "Do they speak English? Last time we met, they only spoke Lupanian."

"No, which is why, Christophe, I'd like you to take care of them."

I blinked. Arthur looked at me, knowing what this meant. Having to chaperone my fifteen-year old cousins meant any opportunity to do any real socializing would be practically nonexistent. I would need to show them around, introduce them to the guests, act as translator… and I didn't even speak any Lupanian.

. . .

"Christophe?" Mother said, waiting for my acknowledgement.

I kept my disappointment inside, as I always did.

"Of course, Mother," I said. "I'd be happy to."

So much for my hopes of meeting anyone special.

MASON

"I don't understand," Mom said, shaking her head. She held the check reverently in her trembling hands. I was afraid she might accidentally rip the thing right in two. "How did you get this money together? I thought we wouldn't be able to pay Mr. Bellock on time…"

"Don't worry about it, Mom," said Jennifer. She crouched down so she could be at Mom's height in her wheelchair, and put her arm around her shoulders. "Mason and I were able to grab some extra work again. Like I told you, you don't need to worry about paying Ackson Bellock his *fee*." Her tone changed at the word, filled with venom.

"That's right," I said evenly. "Jennifer and I have things taken care of."

. . .

"I just don't know how the two of you can be earning this much money. Especially you, Jennifer, you're only sixteen. You're not doing anything… You're treating your body with respect?"

"Hounds of Hell, Mom," Jennifer said, smacking her forehead. "I'm not whoring myself out. Though, Mason on the other hand… Omegas *are* in high demand." She gave me a sly look.

"Muzzle it, Jennifer." I grunted. "I'm doing most of the heavy lifting," I reassured Mom—which was not entirely true. Even though I was four years older than my sister, she was more than able to pull her own weight. "Jennifer is just helping out."

"You shouldn't even be doing any of this," Mom said, tears running down her cheeks. "I'm your mother. I should be taking care of you two."

"No, Mom," I said. "We're a family. We take care of each other."

Mom said, "Come here, honey. Come here," and the three of us embraced.

"Love you, Mom," Jennifer said. "Don't worry. Mason and I will take care of everything."

. . .

A piercing howl from outside interrupted our family moment. Mom groaned, wiped her eyes, and rolled her wheelchair over to the window looking out over the front of our apartment complex.

"That damn homeless prowler is back," she said. "We're paying so much in clan fees, the least they could do is keep this damn neighborhood clean. Oh, he's peeing in the entrance way again." She threw the window open and leaned her head out. "Excuse me!" she shouted. "Leave your mark somewhere else, we don't like having to smell it every time we walk out the door!"

I went over and peeked out the window. On the street three stories below, a disheveled wolf with wild eyes turned its head up to us and let out another deranged howl before shifting back to human form and hobbling off down the street, nearly knocking over a couple of rough looking teenagers who cursed and spat onto the sidewalk after him. A helicopter roared overhead, its searchlight flitting back and forth like an erratic eyeball, and two police cruisers tore down our street with sirens blaring, off to do absolutely dog shit nothing to stop the overflowing crimes that happened every hour of every day in South East Wolfheart. I closed the window.

"Jennifer and I are going to run out for groceries," I said. "We're going to make dinner before I have to head out for my shift."

. . .

"Honey, you don't have to do that. I can get out of this thing to at least cook dinner for us."

"Mom," I said, "we still don't know what's wrong with your legs. Just take it easy, okay? We'll take care of it."

"Please?" Jennifer added.

Mom thought about it and nodded, looking away. The helpless defeat on her face cut into my heart. I hated seeing her this way. She was the strongest woman I knew, besides my little sister. The worst part was that we could barely afford to even get her the wheelchair. The clinics we could afford to take her to could only provide painkillers and a brief examination, which only turned up question marks. Her legs just weren't working right, and shifting into wolf form only made it successively worse, which meant her options for work were now slim to nil.

But maybe… Maybe after tonight, we would finally be able to afford to get Mom some real help, a doctor who could fix it.

Jennifer and I left the apartment building, gingerly avoiding the reeking puddle of wolf piss that stained the wall beneath the mailboxes. Just another beautiful day in the neighborhood.

. . .

"This really is the big one," she said as we turned down the sidewalk, walking close enough so that we could speak at a low volume. We'd gotten really good at it—you never knew when police ears could be trained your way. "Security will be focused on the party. The opportunity will be huge, and we need this. I'm going to be starting school again. We can get Mom some better treatment, and take a break."

"Or not do it anymore at all," I suggested.

She laughed. "I mean, it's good to be optimistic, but let's be real. We agreed to keep it stealth. No more than we really need."

"Right…"

"It does bring up the question. How much longer can we do this?"

"I don't know. But I'm not going to lie, there's a part of me that really likes sticking it to those rich sons of bitches."

"I know," Jennifer said. "Besides. They hardly even miss what we take. How many haven't even realized they've been robbed? What does that say about them?"

. . .

"Yeah," I said. It was all so annoying to think about. The fact that these smug, highborn pieces of trash could live up in their estates, bathing in luxury that they hardly even cared about. It was true. Jennifer and I had infiltrated so many mansions that hadn't even noticed anything was missing. Hell, sometimes we found neat stacks of cash just sitting around on countertops, or precious gemstones in bowls as decorations, like they were candy. "Still… I've been thinking about it a lot, and I think we should stop after this one. Every time we go out we're risking everything, even if it we are taking stuff that's barely detectable."

She stopped walking. "Are you kidding? How will we afford the clan fees? Our living expenses? Mom's medical costs? I'm still in pre-academy, and it's not like you went to an academy or anything. No offense, Mason, but what else could you do for money?"

"I'll find something," I said, annoyed because she was right. I wasn't good at anything—except this. "I'll find another security job. We do this last job, and we do it big. Big enough to hold us over for a while. A fallback while I work."

Jennifer sighed. "We're able to take care of our family this way. We're surviving. You know we're going to struggle to make ends meet any other way, Mason."

Though she wore a stubborn expression on her face, I could see the fear that was hiding just beneath it. Most others would've only seen the face of a tenacious sixteen-year-old, but Jennifer was my sister. I knew exactly how she felt. I went over to a newspaper box with a copy of the *Wolfheart Herald* in the window and pointed to one of the headlines at the bottom of the page.

"Look at this," I said, and read the headline. "Break-ins continue. Blackwood burglar still at large."

She smirked. "They think there's only one of us."

"That's not the point, Jennifer. We've made it to the front page. We've gone months without even being in the paper. Soon enough, we'll be up here." I tapped my finger against the main headline, printed in big bold letters at the top. "And then what?"

Jennifer's expression softened as she digested my words.

"If we get caught, who will take care of Mom?" I asked.

She chewed the inside of her cheek, looked down at the sidewalk, and nodded. "Yeah,"

"Come on," I said. "Let's keep walking."

. . .

We went on down the street, past a homeless red wolf who lay curled up on the sidewalk. He looked up at us and scratched behind his ear with his rear paw, and then asked if we had any spare change. I dug into my pocket and tossed him the few coins that I had.

"You said we should go big," Jennifer said. "What are you suggesting? We take the family jewels or something? Some heirloom?"

"No, we'd never be able to resell something like that. In the house floorplans, there's a dedicated coat room near the front. It's like a whole room where all the guests will be leaving their valuables."

"Right, I remember that. Won't it just be jackets and stuff like that?"

"You'd be surprised. I've worked at parties like this before, and the types of things these people bring in just to show off their money can be ridiculous. But good for us."

At the grocery store, we bought just enough to make a simple soup for dinner. Chicken, beans, tomatoes, collard greens, potatoes… It wasn't much, especially not for two young wolves, but we couldn't afford to buy much else. Most of our money had gone to Ackson Bellock and his fucking "clan fees". In Wolfheart, you were nothing without a clan. You couldn't get work, you couldn't get a place to live. You were an open target. A wolf without a pack couldn't survive.

Our family didn't have much choice for clan membership. We were lowborn. Nothing. The Blood Gulch Clan were a bunch of slimy piles of dog shit, but they were one of the only ones that would accept us, not to mention the only one we could somewhat afford.

"This is delicious, you two," Mom said, smiling as she ate a spoonful of chicken soup. "Thank you for cooking again."

"You're welcome," I said, getting up to clean up my dishes. "I've gotta get ready for work."

"Do they have to have you working that late-night shift?" she asked. "You must be exhausted."

"I'm used to it."

"Oh, Mom," said Jennifer. "I'm going over to Ava's house tonight. We're having a little sleepover. Is that okay?"

"Of course," Mom said. "That's wonderful. You should be going out more, enjoying your vacation. Not working."

. . .

"Thanks, Mom," she said.

I washed my bowl in the sink and went up to my bedroom. I opened the closet and pulled out my loot bag, a special backpack designed to fit me in both human and wolf forms. I put it on the bed next to the old security guard uniform that I used as a cover. From a special compartment cut into the wall in the back of the closet, I pulled out a tablet computer and a small toolkit. I slipped the kit into the backpack and put the tablet on my desk. There was a knock on the door.

"Yeah?"

"It's me," Jennifer said in a low voice.

"Come in."

She entered and shut the door behind her. "Mom is having her glass of wine and watching TV. We won't be bothered."

"Okay," I said, and sat down at the desk. "Take a look."

I powered on the tablet, and Jennifer pulled up a chair next to me. I clicked through the files on the device and pulled up a floorplan for a house. The Luna estate—our target.

. . .

"Okay," she said. "So what's your plan?"

"The front coat room. We enter through the ventilation system leading from the roof, drop in, go through all the guest's belongings stored in there, and slip out. Easy."

"That's it?"

"It'll be easier than sneaking around the house. Everything will be contained to one room."

"I'm not convinced there will be anything worth stealing in there," Jennifer said.

"Just trust me on this one. I've seen someone check in a diamond encrusted handbag before. There will be a bunch of valuable stuff, and how many people are going to this party?"

"From my research, at least a hundred." She thought about it for a moment and then shrugged. "Okay. Let's do it."

"Awesome. Let's go over what we know about the security system and how we're going to access the ventilation…"

CHRISTOPHE

I stood by as my brother Loch and his husband, Tresten, greeted Mother and Father. Tresten held their son Ian in his arms.

"Hello, Ian," Father said. "How's my little grandson? Happy birthday. I've got something special for you later during your party."

"A present?" Ian asked hopefully.

"Yes," said Father, smiling. It was unusual to see him smile, but he couldn't seem to hide it when around Ian.

"What is it?"

. . .

"Patience! You'll find out." He kissed him on the head, and then turned to Loch, his expression straightening. "Loch."

"Dad," Loch said. Father reached out and patted Loch's bicep, like he was appraising it for strength. He nodded to himself, apparently approving. Loch had always been a bit of a black sheep, and even after proving himself by graduating from the Fighting Arts School, he and Father's relationship remained somewhat strained. I knew Father loved him, but being clipped with his emotions towards myself and my brothers was just Father's personality.

"So, I've been told you'll be receiving your master's ranking soon," Father said to Loch. "Congratulations."

"Thanks, Dad," he said.

"I always thought that Tresten would reach master before you."

Loch chuckled. "He probably would've, if not for taking time off due to the pregnancy. He'll be there soon."

"Less than two years, is what I'm hoping for," Tresten added. He put Ian down, and the little boy shifted into his wolf form and started to bound around the room.

. . .

"Ian," I said, "Aren't you going to say hello to your uncles?"

He scampered over to Arthur and me, his paws skidding across the wood floor. "Hi, Uncle Christophe. Hi, Uncle Arthur."

"Hey, little buddy," Arthur said, ruffling the fur on Ian's head. "Are you having fun, now that you're able to shift?"

"It's *great*!" Ian said, jumped around, his tail wagging. Then he sprinted across the room, stopping mid-way to let himself slide. "Wheee!"

Arthur laughed, and I allowed myself a smile. He turned to talk to me as Loch and Tresten caught up with Mother and Father.

"Cute. Can't believe he's already turning four. Still hard to believe that he's Loch's kid. I always figured he and I would be the last of us to get hitched, and he turned out to be the first."

"Who did you think would've been first?" I asked.

"Well… You, I guess." He cocked his head and added, "When we were kids, at least."

. . .

I laughed. "What is that supposed to mean? Are you implying that I've become undesirable?"

"No, not at all. You've been caught up in all your duties for so long, I'm just not sure if you even know how to talk to prospective mates anymore." He stuffed his hands into his pockets and flashed a grin at me.

Damn Arthur and his charms. That grin could put any girl or any omega right in heat. I smiled back stiffly, and he patted my shoulder.

"Funny," I said.

"Just joking, Christophe. I know you don't have much of a choice. Look, don't get down about tonight, alright? There's still a chance you could meet someone. What are you into, anyway? We've never talked much about that."

"I don't really like speaking about those things," I said.

"Why not? We're brothers."

"It's just… It's awkward."

. . .

"Loosen up. C'mon, tell me. Maybe I can guide some your way."

"I'm going to be chaperoning our cousins, remember?"

"Yeah? Some people are into that. You know, mature authority figure? They'll see you're good with kids."

I sighed.

"So," Arthur pressed. "Females? Or males? Betas or omegas?"

I really wasn't in the mood for this kind of conversation. "Don't worry about me, Arthur," I said. "Really. Please."

Ian skidded over and bumped into my leg. "Careful," I said to him, sternly. "You'll get hurt before your party."

"Sorry, Uncle Christophe," he said, his ears drooping slightly, and he scampered away.

"Hey, slow down, kid," Loch said, laughing as he came over to greet us. "Good to see you guys."

. . .

Loch and Arthur hugged, slapping each other on the back. When he moved to me, our embrace was stiff and a little awkward. I loved my brother dearly, but he and I had never seen eye to eye. Being the third alpha, he'd never been the responsible type, and I'd always had to clean up after his messes. It was still hard for me to relate to him.

"Christophe," Mother called, waving me over.

"Yes, Mother?"

"Perennia and Polton Whitefang of the White Tree Clan will be arriving shortly, they're one of the ones who've arranged to stay with us for the night."

"Yes." I nodded.

"They'll be going on to their vacation property up in Diamond Dust afterwards, and Perennia has informed me that she and her husband are transporting some precious and very valuable items. She been very insistent that we allow her to store them securely."

"Okay," I said. "The coat room has a locked door, and we'll have two of our staff manning it the whole night, so…"

. . .

Mother shook her head. "She's insisting we let her use the electronic safe."

I sighed. "If she uses it, all the guests are going to demand access to it."

"I know, I know. Can you help her store her things there, quietly?"

"Yes, of course."

"Thank you, Christophe," she said, and gave me a kiss on the cheek. "Well, I'd better go get ready before everyone starts arriving."

Mrs. Perennia Whitefang was a massive woman, at least three times wider than her balding husband and about three heads taller. When their car pulled up to the front of the house, I was impressed that she was even able to fit into the back of it. The driver hurried around and pulled open the door and she stepped out, dabbing sweat off her forehead despite the car's air conditioning and the day's cool weather. Her husband followed after her, cradling a polished wooden box in his stubby arms.

"Be careful, Polton," she said, looking irritated. "I know how clumsy you can be. Maybe the driver should carry it…"

. . .

"I'll be careful," her husband replied in a squeaky voice. "Benjamin is handling the luggage."

The driver hauled out several huge suitcases from the car's trunk.

"Give him a hand?" I whispered to Stephen, our head of house staff.

"Yes, sir," Stephen replied and rolled out a cart to help the driver with the bags while I went to greet the Whitefangs.

"Mr. and Mrs. Whitefang, welcome to the Luna household. I'm Christophe Luna. How was your drive here?"

"Oh, *dreadful*," Perennia said. She thrust her handbag into my arms and fanned her face. "Have this taken to my room, please."

I held a pleasant smile on my face and showed them inside.

"My parents are just finishing up with some things and will be down to greet you shortly. I'd be happy to give you a quick tour of the house? Mr. Whitefang, my father has told me that you're quite interested in history and genealogy."

. . .

Polton perked up, smiling over the top of the wooden box in his arms.

"You might enjoy our ancestral hall," I continued, "where we have paintings, books, and historical records tracing the lines of the Luna family back—"

"No, no," Perennia said, waving her hand in front of her, like she'd smelled something bad. "We're quite exhausted and would like to be shown to our room so we can freshen up before the party. Now, I've been told that you have a special safe I can use to store my valuables?"

"We do. It's—"

"Good. Take me to it immediately. It's for someone *very* special in Diamond Dust, and they must be given the utmost attention." Her cheeks went rosy pink, while her husband's face flashed with quick irritation. I smiled and nodded. I just wanted get the two of them out of my hair as quickly as possible.

I brought them inside the house and went straight to the storage room we used as a coat room during events. A desk had been installed next to the entrance, where two members of our house staff would be posted to care for our guest's belongings. I punched a pin number into a keypad next to the door, and the lock whirred open. Why she didn't think that was enough security as it was, I had no idea. It wasn't like they were storing their things here long term, and the only guests would be other highborn clan members. No one would be interested in her things, whatever they were.

We used the room normally as a kind of vault to store various things, like records, awards, Mother's extra shoes, and the keys to all the various vehicles we never seemed to use, along with keys to our other properties. The room was lined with recessed shelving along the walls and one long double-sided shelf that ran down the center. About half of the room had been cleared for guest's belongings, and at the back was the electronic safe where the various keys and important documents were kept.

"This is your most secure safe?" Perennia asked. She looked at its gray, metal door down her nose, like she wanted to say that she'd seen better. The truth was that Mother and Father didn't like to store money or anything precious, like jewelry, inside this safe. They had a separate vault for that down in the basement, one that was far more secure, but I wasn't going to say a word about it.

"Yes, Mrs. Whitefang. Your things will be secure here." I punched a pin code into the door, and it swung open. "You can put your box right here." I placed my hand on an empty space on the green velvet lined shelf. "Would you like me to put your handbag in, too?"

. . .

"No, I'd like you to put that in my room, thank you very much," she said, as if it were something I should've known without asking.

Her husband shuffled forward and slid the box onto the shelf, and I closed the safe.

"Will you be checking on it through the night?" she asked as we left the storage room.

I'd learned the art of patience and still mindedness at the Alpha Leadership College, and had dealt with plenty of irritating people—in my position, there was no shortage of them—but I was feeling sore about the party and this woman was starting to really get on my nerves.

"Don't worry, Mrs. Whitefang. The room is very secure, and we'll have two members of our house staff manning it through the night. Now, this is Stephen, our head of staff. He'll show you to your room."

Stephen, who was waiting with the cart of luggage, gave a quick bow. "Right this way, please."

"See you both at the party. If you need anything, Stephen will personally assist you." I nodded a goodbye, turned heel, and quickly escaped.

. . .

I entered the main hall, where workers were still setting up the tables and decor for the party. Getting a glass of something was all that was on my mind at that moment. I'd need it to get through the rest of the day.

"Sir." One of our staff raised his hand and hurried over to me. "Quick question. Mrs. Luna—ah, your Mother—she wanted red flowers for the table centerpieces, but the company made a mistake and delivered white flowers. What should we do?"

"I'm sure white is fine."

"Mrs. Luna seemed very set on having red flowers—"

I stopped walking and took the frazzled man by his shoulders. "You can pass the blame onto me if she does. It's a child's birthday party. White, red, I don't think he really cares. But there is something you can do for me."

"Oh, yes, sir. Anything you ask."

"Find me a drink, please? A strong one."

Soon, I had a glass of bear honey whiskey in my hand, and I fled outside to enjoy it in the one place that nobody would be able to find me. Making my way through the rose garden, I placed the glass onto the ground and, after taking a quick look around, shifted into my wolf form. I gently picked the glass back up with my mouth, and ducked into a space between two hedges that formed a tunnel of crisscrossing vines and branches. Sunlight leaked in through the spaces between the foliage, dappling the ground with pools of shimmering light, like reflections off water. I continued on through the bushes and into the forest until I came out into a grove of apple trees. I shifted back into human form, took a sip of my whiskey, and sighed.

A small stream chuckled along through the trees, and next to it was a large, flat boulder—my boulder. I'd made this place my secret hiding space when I was young, and would sometimes sneak off here when I needed to be alone. It'd been a long time since I'd come here. Time and responsibility just hadn't allowed it, no matter how much I wanted to escape. I sat myself down on the rock and sipped my drink. I should've just brought the whole damn bottle, though drinking too much would definitely not be a good idea. Too many things I'd need to handle tonight.

I was privileged to be the one to handle the family affairs. My father was a respected man, and I would have his position someday. But sometimes I couldn't help but be jealous of my brothers. Loch was married. There wasn't much pressure on Arthur after he'd graduated from the academy, and he was having a grand time fooling around. Vander, being the only omega, got special treatment, and he was up in the north, finding himself.

A journey of self-discovery.

. . .

I couldn't help but laugh. The idea was so foreign to me. The freedom to just up and leave, and have Mother and Father's approval to do so… It was something I would never be able to do.

Not that I needed to. I knew who I was. I was going to lead this family someday. That was what I was destined for.

I closed my eyes and laid back on the rock, spreading my arms out on either side. It felt like I'd been running a marathon, a never-ending marathon, and when was the last time I'd stopped to take a break? A long time. I was tired. And more than that, I felt… empty.

Sunlight filtered through the trees and made glowing spots of red on my eyelids. It was quite chilly in the shade, and the sun was going down. I thought I could smell snow on the air —not here, but miles and miles north, the scent carried down through the wind and on the clouds. A part of me wished I could be away, off in that snow.

My hand absently went down to my thigh, where my birthmark was. Maybe I'd never meet that special someone. Maybe Father was correct—it was all just a bunch of dog shit. People weren't destined or fated to one another. There wasn't someone out there who matched the birthmark, and it was ridiculous of me to keep believing that. I was twenty-seven-years-old. Too old to still believe the stories of old fortune tellers.

. . .

In the end, I'd probably be matched up with someone of my parents' choosing, someone right for the family.

But that was fine. It was just the way things had to be. Like I said, that was what I was destined for. I was okay with that.

But was I really?

My phone buzzed in my pocket, and I sat up and pulled it out.

Shit, it was Mother.

"Hello?"

"Christophe, where are you? Guests are starting to arrive and they haven't even finished putting up the banners yet. Whoever it is we've hired is not doing a very good job."

"I'll be right there, I've just gone out for some air…"

"Well, hurry, please." The speaker crunched as she muffled it with her hand, and I heard her muted voice speaking frantically to someone. "Okay, okay. What? They are? Christophe, your cousins are here."

. . .

The call disconnected, and I stared blankly at the screen for a moment before slipping it into my pocket. I got up, and brushed some dirt off my trousers and shirt. I'd need to change when I got back.

Normally, this hustle and bustle would've energized me. I would not even have thought of going out to take a break, let alone coming all the way out here to the edge of the property, but today I felt different. Maybe it was just because, in a rare occurrence, I'd allowed myself to get my hopes up about tonight.

I downed the remainder of the whiskey, shifted into wolf form, and headed back to the house.

MASON

"Look at all of them," I whispered to Jennifer as I peered through the binoculars from our vantage spot out in the forest. "All of this for some kid's birthday? The way everyone is dressed, you'd think the kid was the king of Wolfheart. Rich bastards."

"I mean, he *is* pretty much royalty," my sister whispered back. "The whole being a Luna and part of the Crescent Moon Clan thing and all."

"I'll never get used to seeing how these people live," I muttered. "I could never understand them. As far as I'm concerned they're all scum." I passed the binoculars to Jennifer. "Things look good. We go around the west side as originally planned. Most of the activity seems to be concentrated in the ballroom area and the outer terrace."

. . .

The words came out bitterly. Just the fact that they had ballrooms and terraces and shit like that pissed me off. Here we were, barely scraping by in our tiny apartment that could probably fit a hundred times or more in just one corner of that damn mansion.

Yeah, I didn't give a flying flea bite about stealing from these people. None of them were redeemable as far as I was concerned.

"Looks like they're doing a birthday toast now, or something," Jennifer said. "They're bringing out a birthday cake. Hounds of Hell, that's the fanciest cake I've ever seen."

"Let me see," I said, and she passed the binoculars over.

I peered into the broad windows looking into the Luna mansion ballroom, where everyone was gathered. Two men wearing white chef's hats were wheeling out a multi-layered cake that was as tall as they were. Standing in the center of the room, the attention focused on them, were two men and a little boy. The birthday boy and his parents, I guessed. I slowly scanned through the rest of the crowd, and paused. A door leading to the outer balcony opened up, and a figure slipped outside, a glass in his hand. It was dark, and I couldn't see him clearly. Apparently, he wasn't interested in participating in the birthday toast. He was alone, and he came up to the stone balcony rail and leaned against it.

. . .

As he did, warm light from the ballroom windows highlighted him, revealing his face. He looked a few years older than me, tall with a well-built but not overly muscular body. His hair was a deep brown, and perfectly styled. He stared out into the distance with the large, red eyes of an alpha, a look of longing on his gorgeous face.

My heart did a flip. I felt a lump form in my throat, and I swallowed to try and get rid of it. It wasn't like I'd never seen a hot alpha male before, but I was immediately drawn in by him. There was just something about him.

None of these rich assholes were redeemable. And yet, suddenly, here was the most attractive man I'd ever laid my eyes on. Almost *painfully* attractive. And what was handsome here thinking about to look so damn melancholic? Hot little rich alpha, sad about his money and mansion and fancy party?

"Hey. Hello?"

"Huh? What?"

I lowered the binoculars. Jennifer was frowning at me. "What do you mean, 'huh'?" she said. "What's going on down there? You've been staring for like five minutes."

"No I wasn't."

. . .

"Yeah, you were. Your mouth was all hanging open, like this." She dropped her jaw, exaggerating.

"Shut up," I said, and tossed the binoculars to her. "I was only scoping out the party. C'mon, let's get going."

Jennifer peered through the binoculars. I thought she was going to spot the guy I was staring at and tease me about it, but she only shrugged and slipped the binoculars into her bag and followed after me.

Just who was he, anyway?

I'd never find out. Better that way. Besides, even though he was hot as hell, I would bet money that he was uptight, spoiled, bratty, and probably terrible in bed too.

I told myself all this and tried to push him out of my mind, but his face was burned into my thoughts.

How could someone who I'd only seen through a pair of binoculars have this kind of effect on me?

Don't worry about it, I thought to myself. *You'll forget about him soon. You're just nervous and excited because of what you're about to do, that's all.*

. . .

Jennifer and I made our way down the tree line and then shifted into our wolf forms. Her dark brown fur easily camouflaged her into the foliage, but my white fur stood out like a beacon and so I had to move carefully, making sure to stay under dense cover at all times. I'd studied books on ancient pack hunting techniques that described how to move silently through terrain and to disguise movements, and Jennifer and I had gotten really good at keeping stealth.

As we came closer to the mansion, the sounds of the party grew louder, and my shifted ears were able to pick up on individual conversations. I filtered through the nonsense they were gabbing about, keeping alert only for signs of detection, though I doubted anyone would notice us. They were all too preoccupied with trying to impress each other, flaunting their wealth and their dog shit successes. It all made me sick.

The main floor of the house was raised about fifteen feet above the ground, so we quickly crossed out of the trees and sprinted up to the side of the building. We paused there for a few seconds, waiting to make sure that things were clear. I nodded to my sister and we moved on, sticking close to the wall. There were windows right above us, and shadows of the people inside played across the ground. We moved towards the balcony, where I knew we would find a ventilation access panel. Clinging to the shadows, the two of us were practically invisible.

. . .

Was he still standing up there? From our position down below, I could only see one small portion of the balcony railing. It was ridiculous, but part of me wanted to see him, just for a moment.

The railing was empty.

I was annoyed at myself for feeling disappointed. I shouldn't have been getting distracted, especially by something so dumb.

In the darkness beneath the balcony just ahead, I could see the small rectangular vent panel that was our in. All we had to do was cross out of the shadows for a brief moment before slipping under the overhanging balcony terrace. Quick and easy, especially with no one here. I motioned to Jennifer with my head—*let's go.*

I moved forward, out of the shadows…

And felt teeth clamp onto my tail. I was suddenly tugged backwards.

Ow, fuck!

It was Jennifer. She'd used her jaws to stop me. I looked back, questioning her angrily with my eyes, and she replied with a silent glance up at the balcony. I followed her look, and winced.

He was standing *right* there.

Somehow, I'd managed get so distracted thinking about him that I hadn't even noticed him come up to the railing. He hadn't seen us. He still had that far off look on his face, and was absently swirling a glass of what looked like whiskey.

We stood as still as statues. *Damn, he was hot.* But this was the closest I wanted to get to him. If he looked down and spotted us, it was game over. We'd have to book it, and everything would be fucked. Last job, busted. No money for Mom's medical treatments. No money to get us through the next few months.

My heart was pounding so hard in my chest, I was worried he'd be able to hear it.

The guy took a sip of his whiskey, and set it down onto the stone railing.

Shit... If he stuck around up there, it'd only be a matter of time before he would spot us. We were well hidden, but not invisible. All it'd take would be a long glance down at the ground below, and there we'd be. I wanted to look back at Jennifer to see how she was taking this, but I was too afraid to make any movements. *The soonest chance we got, we needed to move.*

Then, I heard the balcony door open and the sounds of the party filled the night air. Someone else was coming outside.

"Oh, shit. Christophe! I didn't realize you were out here."

The alpha—Christophe, apparently—turned around, taken by surprise. I watched in horror as his elbow caught the glass on the railing. It spun in the air, spiraling whiskey everywhere, and plummeted down to the ground, where it shattered right at my paws.

One glance, and we'd be spotted.

CHRISTOPHE

When my cousins went to get changed, I took that brief moment of time to grab myself a drink and go out for some air. It was silly of me to believe that I would've had the time to socialize and flirt with anyone, even if I hadn't been in charge of chaperone duty. There were so many things I had to do, to the point where making it across the room and out the door was a miracle in itself.

I drank my whiskey and stared out into the quiet darkness of the forest that surrounded our house. Part of me wanted to jump down from the balcony and run off into the forest to my secret spot, but of course I wasn't going to do that. There was a time in my life when running might've made sense, but that time had passed long ago. I was a grown alpha, and alphas didn't run.

. . .

An alpha faced their destiny with pride and strength, no matter what it was.

And it wasn't like I disliked my course in life. No, I was thankful for the responsibilities and the privilege I had.

It was a quiet night, and the sky was clear and moonless, lit only by a million twinkling stars. It was gorgeous, romantic, the perfect setting for falling in love.

That certainly wasn't my course in life. Not tonight. Probably not any night.

I groaned and made more of my whiskey disappear. I usually didn't get this damn melancholic about things, especially not over something so silly. But here I was, moping. Moping and drinking.

What would happen if I did run? If I just let everything go and left it all behind?

I could do it, just for a night. I could leave this place behind and pretend that I no longer had any responsibilities. I could live like my brothers, free to find my own destiny.

Really, what was stopping me?

. . .

All I had to do was take the leap.

My heart hammered in my chest as I set the glass down on the balcony railing. The dark edge of the forest was calling to me, filling me with a yearning as powerful as the draw of a full moon. I could feel my wolf inside me wanting to be released, struggling to be contained. It wanted to be free, but more than anything else, it wanted to mate.

Hounds of Hell, was that it? Did all this just amount to… being horny?

I snorted.

If that were the case, I could quickly take care of it later tonight in my bedroom.

Behind me, the door suddenly opened and I was enveloped by the noise of the party.

"Oh, shit. Christophe! I didn't realize you were out here."

I swung around to see Arthur standing in the doorway, a pretty girl in a glittering dress on his arm. She looked a little embarrassed; flushed cheeks, like she'd been caught doing something improper.

. . .

"Arthur," I said, with a little smile. "I'll leave you two—"

I heard the pop of shattering glass on the ground below, and realized I'd just dispatched my only friend of the night.

"Shit," I muttered, and leaned over the balcony to look.

Peering down, I saw where it'd broken and made a mental note to have one of the attendants clean it up.

"Sorry about that," Arthur said. "Oh, this is, uh, Miss Melany Dewal of the Rose Claw Clan. Melany, my brother, Christophe."

"Pleased to meet you, Christophe," she said, shaking my hand. "I didn't realize all of the Luna brothers were so handsome."

"Didn't you say you had a sister, Melany?" Arthur asked before sneaking me a wink. " I'm sure Christophe could use some good conversation for the evening."

"I do," she said, "but I can't imagine her being by any kind of substantial dialogue. That is, unless Christophe enjoys keeping ten-year-olds entertained."

. . .

"I—"

At that moment, the door flew open again, and out poured Volk and Lukas Luna, my cousins.

"Christophe!" Volk said in his thick Lupanian accent. "Please, show. We ready! Show! Show!"

I held back a sigh. "Our cousins, visiting from overseas. I have to go." I pushed past my brother and his new friend as I wracked my brain for the tiny bit of Lupanian I'd learned in school. How did I say I needed to get myself a drink? I drew a blank.

"Come on," I said, annunciating slowly. "I need to get myself a drink."

They trailed after me like two pups following the pack leader as I made my way back into the ballroom. Children raced around, weaving through the legs of the adults as they played, and I spotted little Ian in his wolf form chasing around a robotic rabbit, Father's present. I stopped at Julius and Desmond Croc, Ian's grandparents. I turned to my cousins to introduce them to their extended family.

"Um, *rrekvhek*… no, *rrekvhak*." I couldn't remember any damn Lupanian to save my life. "Nevermind. Julius, Desmond, these are my cousins Lukas and Volk, visiting from Lupania."

. . .

"Pleased to meet you both," Julius said. "Lupania. It's a fascinating and beautiful country. Did you know it has some of the best healers in that side of the world? What do you both intend to study when you're older?"

My cousins looked at me, puzzled.

"Ah, they don't speak much English," I told Julius. "My parents have assigned me as their translator, which was a bit of an oversight seeing as how I've only ever taken one class of Lupanian."

"Oh," said Julius. "Well, you know who might be able to help you a bit? Mr. Polton Whitefang. He speaks Lupanian quite well. Desmond, have you seen him?"

"Of course, I have," his husband replied with his trademark, louder-than-intended voice. "Last I saw him, he was in the smoking room. I wanted to talk to him but it seemed like he'd already had a few too many, uh…" He made a drinking motion with his hand. "I don't know if he'd be of any help to you, Christophe."

"I guess I'm willing to take that chance," I said, glancing over at my cousins, who had deer-in-the-headlights looks on their faces.

. . .

I led my cousins towards the smoking room, stopping to greet a few more guests. I decided against finding that replacement drink. Walking around with a glass constantly in my hand might not make a good impression on younger minds.

My father used the smoking room to meet with clients and important clan members, and tonight it was the place where the adults could go to get away from the children's festivities. No kids allowed, and that included my two cousins. I felt bad having to leave them in the hallway, especially because I wasn't sure if I was telling them to "wait here" in Lupanian or to "get wasted", but any moment out of chaperone duty was a welcome one.

The large, circular room was lined with Luna family curios, including three huge portraits of three alpha ancestors from five generations past. They stared down with stern judgement, their watchful eyes always assessing the quality of their descendants. As a child, this room intimidated me. It was the place I was seldom allowed to enter, and when I did, their eyes were always on me, questioning my worth as an alpha Luna.

Tonight, the room had an uncommonly jovial atmosphere, and it bustled with the guests wanting an escape from the noise of the youngsters outside.

"Mr. Whitefang," I whispered to the attendant at the door. "Is he here?"

. . .

"Yes, sir. Just on the opposite end of the room, by the drinks. Would you like me fetch him for you?"

"No, that's alright. Thank you."

Polton Whitefang stood out like a black wolf on a snowbank. He was slumped into a leather easy chair, his balding head shimmering with sweat and his eyes listlessly scanning the room as he clutched a glass of something in both hands. He looked up at me when I walked up to him, and I could immediately see that Desmond was right—he wasn't going to be of any help to me.

"Mr. Whitefang," I said, taking the seat next to him. "I just wanted to check in with you to give you my reassurances that your belongings are secure. Are you doing alright? Would you like me to get you some water?"

"I dun giveadamn about those damn rocksss," he slurred. He reached out to place his glass down onto an imaginary side table, and I quickly caught it in my hand when he let go. He put his arm around my shoulder and leaned into me. "Buh thanks. I appreciate it, young man. Well, my wife will. Issall she damn cares about, those damn gems. Oh, what'rr y' drinking?"

. . .

He pointed at the glass in my hand—his glass—and then took it from me and started to sip from it.

"Ah, let me get a new one for you, Mr. Whitefang," I said, taking the glass back from him. I stood and caught the eye of the attendant, who hurried over. "Get him a water and have someone help him to his room," I said.

"Yes, sir."

"Y'know," Polton Whitefang said, grabbing my shoulder and pulling me back into the chair. "Issreally all she cares 'bout. Alpha's eyes, they're called. And y'know who they're for?"

"No," I said, really not interested in hearing about his wife's things.

"Johnathan Burnside."

The way he said that name sounded like he was on the verge of vomiting. "I'm afraid I don't know who that is," I told him.

"No," he said. "Course not. Y'wouldn't. You'd only know if you were taking skiing lessons at the damn Diamond Dust resort."

. . .

"I see," I said. Dammit, I wasn't here to listen to his marital problems. I glanced around the room. It was obvious people were avoiding looking over here so that they didn't get roped into interacting with Polton. Where was that attendant?

"Right under my nose!" Polton said, slapping my arm. "She doesn't even give a damn."

"I'm sorry," I said. I didn't know what else to say.

"We've been going up to that damn resort almost every damn week. All the *gifts!* And why must *I* be there?"

I made a noncommittal noise and gave him my most reassuring smile. His eyes were glassy and seemed to look through me. Finally, the door opened and the attendant came in with a bottle of water on a tray and…

Oh, *dammit*.

With Perennia Whitefang in tow.

"Water, sir," the attendant said, handing the bottle to Polton. "If you'd come with me, we've arranged a quiet room for you."

. . .

"I'd prefer *not!*" Polton cried, throwing his finger into the air. "I'm fine *righhere!*"

"Polton, you're drunk!" Perennia hissed, grabbing his arm. "You're making a fool of yourself. Go with this man! Go!"

She yanked him to his feet. I was expecting him to put up some kind of fight and throw a drunken scene, but to my surprise he was immediately silenced, like a shamed puppy. The attendant took him by the arm and helped him out the room, not without a few stumbles.

"My apologies for my husband," Perennia said.

"Not a problem at all. If you'd excuse me, I need to—"

"Ah, I'd like it if you'd take me to the secure room to check on my belongings. Just to make sure everything's in order."

"I assure you, Mrs. Whitefang, everything is secure. The room is locked and being watched as we speak."

"Locked and watched by whom, Christophe? By whom? I don't know these men. They could be anyone, they could be thieves."

. . .

"Most of the house staff have been with my family since before I was born, madam," I said. "And an insult to my family is an insult to the Crescent Moon Clan."

Perennia's mouth opened and closed like a fish gulping for air, and in the end, she crossed her huge arms over her chest and huffed a barely-there apology.

"We'll go down to the room and check on your things, and once you see that everything is fine I ask that you please trust the security and enjoy the rest of the party. Agreed?"

She huffed again and nodded. I smiled.

"Please, follow me."

MASON

⤺

*B*ack in human form, I pulled the vent grate closed behind us and followed Jennifer as she crawled towards the pitch black darkness of the ventilation duct. My heart was racing. We would've been caught if it hadn't been for that half a second window of opportunity when he'd turned his back to us.

We stopped and activated small headlamps that just barely illuminated the passage ahead. Couldn't take any chances with light leaks that might give us away.

"Ready?" Jennifer whispered over her shoulder.

"Let's fucking do it," I said, and we made our way forwards, slowly and silently.

. . .

The ventilation system was a maze that snaked its way throughout the entire house, and we'd memorized the path we needed to take to get to our destination. Still, despite the preparation, it was a little nerve-wracking to move only by memory, never having actually been here before. Was there someone walking in the hallway next to us or below us, just a few feet away? Were we being quiet enough? Jennifer and I had always been skilled at moving quickly and quietly, ever since we were kids. We'd outran and escaped the bullies in our apartment building enough times to the point where they stopped trying to catch us. We'd tested our abilities plenty of times during our little heists. Despite all that, it never got any less exhilarating.

Jennifer and I should've given this up a long time ago. Maybe that was why we hadn't.

Our lights gleamed off of the sheet metal as glowing specks of dust drifted in front of my eyes like fireflies. We both kept our ears shifted to wolf form so that it'd be easier to pick up any signs of detection. Even though we were beneath the first floor, I could still hear the party up on the floor above us, a constant rhythm of dull thudding as people moved around. Slowly, it grew quieter as we moved away from the ballroom area.

After five minutes of crawling we reached what first looked like a dead end, but was actually where the ventilation shifted ninety degrees vertically, taking us up into the ceiling of the first floor where we'd eventually be above our destination. Almost there.

. . .

Jennifer stood up straight in the vertical shaft and raised her right foot. I crawled forward and secured her foot on my right shoulder, holding her ankle tightly with my hand. We paused for a moment, listening.

"Coast is clear," I said. "I don't hear anyone."

"Yeah," she replied, and boosted herself up so she was standing on both my shoulders. I brought my knees forward and got to my feet, lifting her up into the passageway. She then grabbed the edge of the horizontal vent above us and hauled herself up.

Her voice drifted back down to me. "Do you need the rope?"

I tilted my head back. The cross vent was about six feet up, not too far. I could make the jump, but I had to be careful to do it with as little movement as possible to not give us away.

"I can do it," I said.

The space was cramped. I didn't have enough room to swing my arms for extra jump momentum. I'd need to have them already extended above me, like a diver jumping into a pool, and make the jump that way. I rubbed my hands together, took a deep breath, and bent my knees until they touched metal. Then, with a sharp exhale, my feet left the ground.

Shit! Not enough!

My fingers hooked the edge but immediately began to slip. I was going to fall!

My right hand gave way first, and the left just a half second later. I must've actually been hovering in the air for a split second before Jennifer's hands shot out and grabbed my wrist. My body swung forward, and I stopped myself from impacting against the side of the vent with my free hand. A low, hollow *dong* vibrated through the vent. I cringed. Not as bad as it could've been, but still.

Jennifer pulled me up and I hooked the ledge and hauled myself the rest of the way. She gave me a look.

"Thanks," I told her.

"Next time, use the rope," she said, and kept crawling.

As we moved along, my mind wandered back to the man I'd seen standing on the balcony. The idea of who he was—a spoiled, rich brat with absolutely no worries in life except for how much money was left in his bank account—pissed me off. Standing up there, moping around with his expensive whiskey and his stupid suit. Dammit. I had no idea who he was and I hated him.

But the thing I hated the most about him was how attractive he was. No, how attractive *I* found him. That was on me. I could've just put him completely out of my mind, but his handsome face stuck there, refusing to leave, teasing me. I wanted a better look at him. I wanted to see his face again so that I could pick out some flaw and forget about him.

He's one of them. *What else is there to find?*

For some reason, that wasn't enough to make me forget about him.

Jennifer stopped, and I nearly rammed my face into her heels. She looked over her shoulder at me and pointed at the floor. *Here*.

I nodded.

She crawled forward a few more feet, revealing a ventilation panel that was rimmed with light leaking through from the room below. She turned herself around at the opposite side of the panel, and we both peered down through the grating to see a creamy marble floor. I closed my eyes and shifted out my wolf's nose.

. . .

Smelled good, sounded good. I could hear people talking outside, but the room was empty. I nodded to Jennifer, and we removed the panel and pushed it off. Light filled the duct, and Jennifer clicked off her headlamp. She turned herself around again, and then slid forward and slipped down, dropping into the room. I magnetically secured a line to the vent opening and then followed after her.

Jennifer was taking in everything with wide eyes. I grinned at her and made a thumbs up. *Jackpot*. The room was lined with shelves and racks filled with belongings. There were at least two dozen handbags, several of which looked like there were studded with diamonds. Fur coats, jackets, and even a few weekend duffle bags. No matter what, this was a *haul*. A major haul.

We both slipped our backpacks off, unzipped the sides to expand them, and set to work. Jennifer went to the purses and handbags, and I went to the coats. We worked silently, not knowing how much the people on the other side of that door would be able to hear.

Hounds of Hell, the *things* these people brought in with them. Several of the men's jackets had clips of cash stuffed into the breast pocket that totaled more in value than some of our entire hauls. There were solid gold pens, a cigarette lighter that probably cost as much as a car, and even more cash. The guys really liked to carry wads of cash with them, apparently.

. . .

I made my way down the row towards the back of the room, my bag already near capacity.

"I'm full," Jennifer whispered, grabbing the line hanging from the ceiling. "You good?"

I stuffed a pair of fur gloves into my bag and zipped it up—and then saw it. "Whoa. This wasn't on the map."

A safe.

I went over to it and looked at the keypad on the door. Jennifer came up next to me.

"It's electronic. Have you ever tried opening one of these ones?" I asked her.

"Yeah," she said, "but I've only done it a couple times, and I don't know how long—"

"Did you bring your gear?"

"Of course."

"We've got some extra time, let's see what's inside."

. . .

She frowned, and then set her pack on the ground. "I don't think this is a good idea."

"We have time," I repeated. We'd only been there for less than five minutes.

"Fine," she said, and pulled out a small pouch from her bag.

While she worked, I went over to the door to keep an ear out for anyone coming. The coast was still clear and wide open. Nobody would know we'd been here until the party was over, and even then, they probably still wouldn't realize they'd been robbed.

"Did I bring my wad of cash with me tonight, honey?"

"Oh, I don't know."

"I guess not."

Ten minutes passed. Then fifteen.

I started to pace the room.

. . .

We still had time. At this point, we could probably be here all night without anyone finding us.

"Stop that," Jennifer said. "You're screwing with my head."

"How much longer?" I asked.

"I don't know. It depends on the firmware of the system. We *could* just leave, you know? We didn't expect this."

"I know, I know. But… It's our last job. Come on, I thought you of all people would want to know what's inside there."

"I do, but… I'm just not used to sticking around for so long. Wait. Wait, I got it. It's gonna open."

"Yes! Jennifer, you're amazing."

I hurried over. The panel on the safe flashed green as a series of numbers scrolled across the screen, and we leaned in eagerly. The string of scrolling numbers began to stop, one column at a time, until it was down to one final digit.

"Here we go," Jennifer whispered.

. . .

The number stopped. The panel turned red.

And then a siren started, as loud as a howl to the moon.

We looked at each other. Jennifer's eyes were wide.

We both spoke at once.

"*Shit.*"

"How do you shut it off!" I shouted.

"I don't know! We gotta get out of here!"

She grabbed her bag from the floor and ran to the escape rope with me on her heels. I skidded over to a chair sitting in the corner, and jammed it under the door handle just as I heard the lock release. The door pushed forward and wedged against the chair and through the opening came the confused shouts of the people on the other side. Shoulders immediately started to slam against the door.

"Christophe, come on!" Jennifer shouted. She was already half way up the rope.

. . .

"Go!" I shouted back, and she shimmied her way up and disappeared into the vent. I ran and jumped for the rope, hauling myself up as quickly as I could. Jennifer looked down at me with wide, frightened eyes.

The door vibrated with a heavy kick, again and again. I reached the vent and Jennifer grabbed at my wrists, struggling to pull me in. I couldn't move! I was stuck!

"The bag!" Jennifer screamed. "It's caught!"

Swollen with loot, it was caught against the opening. In a moment of panic I strained and pulled, but it was useless. I knew I had no other choice. Still holding on to the ledge, I released one hand at a time and let the bag fall from my shoulders. It hit the ground and burst, the goodies inside scattering across the floor just as the door exploded open.

I looked over my shoulder and saw two men in suits—part of the house staff—staring back at us in shocked disbelief. Then *he* showed up.

"What the hell is going on?" he shouted. A woman arrived behind him, saw the mess inside, and let out a high-pitched squeal of a scream.

My eyes met his for the first time. His gaze pierced mine and an electric thrill coursed through my entire body.

. . .

One final pull, and I disappeared up into the vent.

"Go, go, go!"

We crawled as fast as we could, banging along the inside of the duct, praying that they didn't have the system memorized like we did.

Shit. I'd gotten cocky and greedy, and I had no idea if we were going to be able to get out of this. At least they hadn't seen Jennifer.

I strained to listen to their movements—they could hear us, they were following us.

"The moment we get out of that vent, I want you to run," I said. "Drop your bag, shift, and run. I'll be right behind. You got that?"

"What, are you crazy? I'm not going to drop my bag."

"They only know about me. We can't risk them coming after you, too. Get out of here as fast as you fucking can. I'll take the pack."

. . .

"Mason…" I could hear the fear in her voice. Jennifer was tough, but she was just a kid. We'd never been in this situation before.

"Do what I say, Jennifer," I said, doing my best to sound calm. "We'll be fine."

We dropped down the vertical shaft. Almost there. I couldn't hear them anymore, but I knew they'd be outside, searching all of the ventilation access panels. It was a huge house, so maybe, just maybe, we'd get lucky.

I couldn't let them get Jennifer. For Mom's sake. She couldn't find out that Jennifer had been doing this.

Jennifer quickly undid the screws on the access panel and pushed it open. I could hear the party upstairs in commotion, the voices of the guests trying to figure out what was going on. She reluctantly removed her pack, and handed it to me.

"You go straight for the woods, before anyone thinks to look here. I'll go around the way we came and meet you there. It's better we split up. Go!"

She nodded, and in seconds was in her wolf form, sprinting through the darkness away from the house. I shifted too, white fur covering my body as my muscles expanded and my bones reconfigured. Jennifer disappeared into the tree line, and turned to move alongside the house.

"Hey, you! Stop!"

I turned and saw him—Christophe—standing up on the balcony, pointing down at me. Funny how quickly I went from wanting to get a better look at him to wishing he never existed. Funny how *he* of all people would be the one to come after me. Who the hell was he, anyway? Head of security?

I bolted, and immediately felt icy sharp pain shoot up my paw. A yelp escaped my mouth as my leg buckled and I somersaulted across the dirt. When I righted myself, I saw that I'd stepped right onto the broken whiskey glass. I didn't know how bad the cut was, but I knew I was bleeding. I gritted through the pain and ran.

Behind me, I heard an impact on the dirt.

Fuck! He was fucking chasing me!

It felt like molten fangs were being driven into my paw every time it made contact with the ground, but I refused to slow down. I chanced a look over my shoulder and saw him in hot pursuit, a huge black wolf with intense red eyes. He was on me, his body pointed and focused, like a fighter jet. The crazy thing was that I was still somehow faster than him. I was in better shape than him, but that didn't mean I could relax. I was putting some distance between us, but how long could I keep up this pace?

I snapped the strap of my pack with my teeth, clipping it loose, and then tossed it back at my pursuer in a lame attempt to create some kind of obstacle. Plus, it was slowing me down. It was painful to dump it, but I had to.

Fuck me. Empty handed. I fucked up. This was what happened when you got greedy.

The mansion was far behind us now. I skirted along the edge of the forest, the sound of my heart pounding loudly in my ears. I didn't have to look, I could feel him behind me, slowly gaining. Every step was agony. It felt like a shroud was being draped around me, darkness closing in, pinholing my vision. Forward. Forward. I just needed to outlast him. I had to get home. I had to get to Jennifer. I couldn't let him catch me.

Maintain, Mason. Keep going.

I veered into the woods and weaved between the trees, bounding over falling logs and ignoring the bolts of pain that cut into my leg.

Don't stop.

. . .

You can do this.

Branches caught my fur, like claws trying to drag me down to the ground. The trees whipped by like signs on a highway. It felt like my legs were carrying me on their own, like I was no longer in control. The only thing I cared about was getting away, and getting my sister back home safely. We'd figure the money out... We'd find a way to survive.

I'll never do this again. This was the last time.

It was a promise that I released to the cosmos, to whoever might be listening, and the reply I got was not what I had hoped for.

As I hurdled over a downed tree, my injured leg seized up and gave way under me, sending me tumbling to the ground. When I tried to get back on my paws, white hot pain seared through my body, nearly pulling consciousness from me. I collapsed again, and for the first time I saw the gash running down the center of my paw. I felt like I was about to faint. Then I realized that I was alone.

A breeze whistled through the trees, rustling the foliage and swirling a curl of dead leaves up from the ground. Slowly and gingerly, I got to my feet, careful not to put pressure on my paw. My white fur was soaked red.

. . .

I needed to find Jennifer. I needed to—

Suddenly, he exploded from the thicket, a mass of black fur and hard muscle that I only caught a flash of before he slammed into me. I felt the breath vacuumed from my lungs from the impact, and I hit the ground. There was no way I'd be able to get back up, even if he weren't pinning me down with his forepaws. He stood over me, teeth bared in an angry snarl. I wanted to fight him, to teach him how things were done in my neighborhood, but I could hardly move. I could hardly think. The tunnel was closing around me, and I was fading fast.

Sirens cut through the silence of the forest.

All I could do was pray that Jennifer had escaped unnoticed.

CHRISTOPHE

I watched the police load the omega into the back of the ambulance while party guests gawked from their cars as they left. Strapped onto a stretcher and still in wolf form, the stubborn idiot had refused to shift back to his human form, even though it would've helped them heal the nasty wound he'd gotten from where I'd dropped that fateful whiskey glass.

If he'd succeeded with his little heist, he would've made off with an incredible amount of money and valuables—two full bags' worth—including Perennia Whitefang's precious gifts. She was furious, of course, and if it hadn't been for her relatively lower status she probably would've made a larger scene than she had. Her husband seemed amused about the whole thing, just watching quietly with a smile on his face. They'd left not too long after the police showed up, with Perennia saying she no longer felt safe in our home. I didn't try to stop her.

. . .

Still—she had a valid reason to feel unsafe. I couldn't believe that we'd been robbed. Even though we had a state of the art security system, he'd managed to bypass everything by slipping into the air conditioning system, and to make things worse, the coat room didn't have any kind of monitoring system inside it. There'd just never been a reason for it. There were acres and acres of wild forest on every side of our home, and that was security in itself.

"The guy knew what he was doing," Loch said. He, Arthur, and I stood in the now-empty coat room, and I went over to the safe and examined it. Nothing of ours had been disturbed.

"Obviously," I said. "He knew how to access this room. He must've had information about the house."

"Not to mention he was able to crack the safe," Arthur said. "Is this the same thief that hit the Blackwood District?"

"I wonder," I said. "The Blackwood thief never stole anything big, though. Nothing on this scale. Though they had to be as well prepared as this guy was, to be able to get away with being undetected for so long."

"I bet they're the same," Loch said.

"Christophe."

. . .

We all straightened at the sound of Father's voice. He was standing in the doorway of the coat room, his hand on the door frame. The door hung loosely on one hinge, broken after I'd kicked it down.

"Yes, Father?"

"Come with me."

I followed him out of the room. I couldn't shake the feeling of smallness, like I was a child again and Father was about to reprimand me for my mistakes. And I had made a lot of mistakes. Making sure the party went smoothly had been my responsibility, and even though the incident wasn't my fault, I could've arranged for better security. Also, after leaving them alone, my two little cousins had gone off and somehow managed to get their hands on some bear honey whiskey, so we not only had upset guests, a stain on our reputation, and a broken door, we also had two drunk kids vomiting in the bathroom. Thankfully, Mother volunteered to care for them. She seemed shaken by the break-in, and I think she needed something to take her mind off of it anyway.

"You did well," Father said, and I looked at him in surprise.

"Thank you, Father," I replied. "I don't feel the same way."

. . .

"It was an unfortunate situation that could've happened regardless of the preparation. You took care of everything, and not to mention, you caught the thief."

We walked out to the front of the house, where a police crew was milling about out and around the property collecting evidence. Father put his hand on my shoulder. "You are ready to lead this clan," he said. "Just as you've been to destined to."

"Thank you, Father." For some reason, his words didn't make me feel as much pride as I would've expected them to.

"I'm granting you full clan powers on this matter," Father continued, with a smile. "Follow up with the chief inspector about this situation."

Now I *really* was shocked. Full clan powers. That meant he was giving me permission to act on his behalf.

"Put the thief behind bars, or have him exiled. Your judgement, I leave the decision to you."

"Yes, Father," I said.

He squeezed my shoulder and went back inside, leaving me standing alone outside. The police were spraying down the path the thief had taken, where his injured paw had left a trail of bloody paw prints. I traced the trail back towards the house, the prints now nothing but a smeared haze of rust-colored water. I stopped at the side of the house, near where he'd stepped on the broken whiskey glass. The glass had been cleaned up, brushed away along with all the other evidence that anything had taken place here tonight. Soon, everything would be back to normal. The house security would be upgraded, we'd send condolence gifts to all of the guests, and everything would be forgotten.

It was now my responsibility to deal justice to the scumbag who decided it'd be a good idea to steal from the Lunas.

I leaned my back against the wall, feeling the sudden weight of this new responsibility. These were the kind of decisions I'd be making as clan leader. Real things. Deciding the fate of people who betrayed the rules of the clan, or those who crossed us. Determining what was best for not just my family, but for an entire clan. Hundreds and hundreds of people.

Now I really felt like I could use that drink.

I sank down onto my haunches and buried my face into my palms. I needed to hold it together. Of course things weren't going to be easy. I never expected them to be.

Through the cracks of my fingers, I saw something on the ground that nearly made my heart stop. I leaned forward to get a better view of the single bloody paw print that the cleaning crew had missed. It stood out to me, because I knew that print as well as I knew my own. Was I imagining it? It couldn't be possible, could it? But no, it really was there, right down to the single missing pad. It was the same paw print that I'd carried on my right thigh since birth. My fated mate mark.

* * *

I sat in the now empty smoking room, the smell of the party still lingering in the air, a mix of perfume, cologne, and hors d'oeuvres. Sinking into the armchair, I swirled a glass of whiskey in my hand and occasionally brought it to my lips. A fire crackled in the fireplace in front of me, and the portraits of my ancestors looked down at me. I felt remarkably like Father in that moment, something that was oddly disturbing to me. Everything about this day had gotten me out of sorts.

My thoughts took me back to when I'd kicked open the door to the coat room and saw him about to disappear into the ceiling. I hadn't given much thought to how he'd looked at the time, but now I was wracking my brain, trying to remember every detail of his face. It came as a blur. He was handsome, I did remember that, with pale hair and intense blue eyes. He looked young. Definitely younger than I was. He was an omega; his eyes and fur gave that away. He was a criminal and thief, and also the owner of that paw print.

Fated mate marks aren't real.

. . .

I felt numb. I wanted to believe that it was a coincidence. There had to be thousands, perhaps millions of wolves with a missing pad on their paw, and it just so happened that I had a birthmark that carried that appearance. Something deep inside me knew that wasn't the case, though. I could feel it in my gut, that it was *real*.

Hadn't I wanted to believe it was real? Why was I trying to convince myself differently now?

What did it mean?

The door to the smoking room creaked as it opened, jerking me out of my thoughts. I looked over my shoulder and saw it was Arthur. He walked over to the liquor table and poured himself a glass of whiskey out of one of the crystal decanters, and brought it over to the chair next to me. He groaned as he sat down.

"What a night, huh? I was this close, Christophe. This close." He held up his hand, measuring an inch with his thumb and forefinger. "The daughter of the leader of the Golden Forest Clan. *So* hot. Refined, with a naughty streak. You don't meet many like that very often. Of all the nights we had to get fucking robbed."

I breathed a laugh through my nose that was more just a mild acknowledgement. My thoughts were as far away from Arthur's girl problems as they could get.

. . .

"She asked me if there was a room we could be alone in, and I just said 'pick one.' We were going for it, and the alarm went off. I could've just—"

"Arthur?"

"What?"

"Do you believe in fated mates?"

He laughed. "For some people, maybe. Not me, though. I believe in… Fated mates for the night."

"Even if you had a fated mates marking? What would you do?"

He gave me a look. "*You* were told that you have one, and you don't believe in that nonsense. Though, I guess if someone showed up bearing my mark, that'd be something. That certainly could be a mind changer. If I knew that person existed, I'd never stop until I met them." He shrugged. "Or not. Why are you asking me this? You didn't meet someone tonight after all, did you?"

I shook my head. "No."

. . .

"Mm." He swallowed his drink in one gulp. "Too bad. Nice job running that asshole down today, by the way. You were on him for nearly a mile. I'm impressed. Didn't know you had that kind of stamina."

Arthur stared at me, waiting for me to retort, but I wasn't interested.

"Father tasked me to zip up the situation," I said.

"No surprise."

"He gave me full clan authority," I added.

His eyes widened. "Damn. First time, huh?"

"Yeah."

"What are you going to do?"

"I don't know. I've never had someone's fate in my hands before."

. . .

"I know Dad would make an example of him. Exile. Or worse."

He stood and patted my shoulder. "Gotta say, Christophe. I'm glad I'm not in your shoes. I don't know how you handle all that pressure. I've got a lot of respect for you."

"Mm."

Arthur left, returning me to the solitude of my thoughts. No, solitude wasn't right. *He* was there, at the center of my thoughts. This man who I didn't know. This omega. This criminal.

The mark on my leg seemed to tingle, like it'd been touched with static electricity. I straightened my pants and brushed my thigh with my palm, unsure if it'd only been my imagination. That paw print. His paw print. It couldn't be real. I was convincing myself of false things because I'd been feeling discontent lately. It was just a coincidence, it had to be. How could it be possible to be marked from birth? That kind of magic might've existed a long time ago, but not today. Not anymore.

I swallowed down the rest of my whiskey and started to pace the room. Visiting the guilty in person wasn't required of me, not for something like this. I could make a phone call to the chief inspector and tell him what the Crescent Moon Clan's decided punishment would be. Almost certainly, the kind of person who went around breaking into houses wouldn't have the backing of any clan of influence, so there'd be no disputes, no argument.

But I needed to know. I *needed* to see him, and hopefully put this stupid thing to rest.

Donning my jacket, I passed Stephen in the main hall. He was with two of our house staff, the three of them pushing carts of empty champagne glasses.

"I'm taking the car, Stephen," I said.

"At this hour, sir?"

"I'm going downtown."

"Yes, sir… Would you like me to drive you?"

"No. I won't be long. Oh, and Stephen?"

"Sir?"

"Keep this from my parents."

. . .

He nodded. "Certainly."

I roared towards downtown Wolfheart, taking the special restricted roads reserved only for high clan officials. The brightly lit tunnels passed through mountainsides and snaked deep underground, bypassing the crowded freeways and packed streets of the city. A short while later I took the exit that put me right at the police compound, and drove up a ramp to an elevator platform which brought the car into the compound's parking garage. Chief Inspector Burnside himself hurried out to greet me.

"Mr. Luna, I didn't know to expect you tonight."

"It's an unexpected visit," I said.

"I'm guessing you're here to see the man who broke into your mansion?"

"That's right."

I followed him through the compound, which despite the hour still bustled with life as officers worked. I saw a muzzled grey wolf with a scarred face getting hauled away by two officers, one in human form and one in wolf form. He was dragging his paws, doing everything he could to make moving him difficult, and eventually he even lifted a leg and started to urinate on the wall. The officers shouted and yanked the chain connected to a collar around his neck, and he let out a strained yelp. I looked away.

"Is this your first time at the compound, Mr. Luna?" Chief Inspector Burnside asked. "I've only ever met with your father."

"It is."

"Well, welcome to the dog pound. Probably a shock, coming here from your world. You get used to it. By the way, let me thank you for the donations made from your clan. We really appreciate your assistance."

"Certainly," I said, distracted. I didn't want to schmooze, I wanted to see *him*. "So, what do you know about this man? What's his name?"

"He didn't turn up in any of our databases. This is the first time he's been caught. We don't know his name, but it's only a matter of time. Don't worry."

"I'll ask him."

The Chief laughed. "Be my guest, but I doubt he'll tell you anything. Right through here."

. . .

He placed his hand on a wall scanner, unlocking a door in front of us with a loud buzz. Inside was a long row of cells closed off with thick glass walls. Unsavory characters paced or sat in them, some in human form, some in animal form. I made eye contact with a huge bear with mangy fur who then stood up off of his comically small cot and towered up to the ceiling. We reached the final cell. In it was a man curled up on his cot with his back to me, a blanket pulled over him. Compared to the people in the other cells, he seemed out of place. Even though I couldn't see his face, there was just that air about him. He looked small. Vulnerable. I felt a strange tug in my chest. My heart was pounding.

"Wake up in there," the Chief said, and pressed a button that sounded a loud buzzing noise inside the cell. The man jerked and bolted upright. Slowly, he turned around. He cradled his right hand, which was wrapped up in a white bandage. He stood up, and the blanket slid from his shoulders, revealing that he was naked down to the waist, his small frame carved with muscles. It was no wonder why he was able to outrun me, even with a hurt paw. His powerful physicality was obvious.

He narrowed his glowing sapphire eyes at me, and I felt my heart start to race a little faster. He was gorgeous.

His voice emerged, a low growl from his throat.

"You."

MASON

The buzz of the alarm jolted me out of my thoughts. I wasn't sleeping—there was no way I'd be able to fall asleep with everything that was on my mind. I was worried about Jennifer. I was pretty sure she'd gotten away undetected because the police still seemed to believe I'd been alone, but now Jennifer was by herself. And what would she tell Mom? Eventually they'd figure out who I was. Would Jennifer be safe? Would they find out she was involved?

I couldn't stand to think of Mom finding out what I'd been doing, let alone the both of us.

I'd really fucked up, bad. I'd gotten cocky. I'd come up with all the precautions to keep us safe, and in the end, it was me who'd decided to ignore them. If only I'd just ignored that damn safe…

. . .

The worst part was that we had nothing to show for it. And if they found out we were responsible for the Blackwood robberies…? What would happen to Mom if Jennifer and I were no longer around? She had no one else.

It was hot in the cell, so I'd removed my shirt. My right hand throbbed painfully beneath the bandages. They told me that it would take more time to heal because of how badly I'd mangled it in my attempt to escape.

"Wake up in there."

What the hell did they want at this hour? Was this part of their interrogation game? Never ending questioning, no time to rest?

I turned, and was shocked at who I saw standing with the chief inspector.

What was he doing here? *Christophe*. That was his name. I'd thought he might've been on the security team or something like that, but seeing him again now changed my mind. He didn't have that vibe. And judging from the immaculate way he dressed… He was someone important.

Damn. Was he a Luna?

. . .

With that realization came a much heavier one. If he was an alpha Luna, then that meant he had a direct influence on what my punishment would be.

"You," I said.

He looked like he was judging me, looking down at me, and it pissed me off. And I hated that I still found him attractive, even after all of this. It was like my body and my mind were clashing with each other. He looked fucking perfect, especially seeing him up close, almost overwhelmingly so. I felt a deep, aching hunger inside, like I wanted to eat him up. I could feel blood rushing to my cock, and I did everything I could to fight away the fantasies that had begun to swirl around in my head. This smug son of a bitch was the enemy. And he was the reason why I was sitting in this damn cell.

He straightened his cuff links and said something to the chief, who nodded and left us alone. We glared at each other, a thick silence settling between us. The man standing on the other side of the glass seemed to be slightly different from the one I'd spied on the balcony. That one had been lost in his thoughts. I remembered seeing something in his eyes, a longing for something that'd piqued my curiosity. There was none of that here, now. This man was all business.

"My name is Christophe Luna," he said, his voice a velvety baritone that I could feel even through the glass that separated us. "First alpha of the Luna family."

. . .

So, he was a Luna, the first alpha.

"Given I just introduced myself, it'd be the polite thing to give your name, too."

I looked at the ceiling and scratched my nose with my middle finger. He snorted. Was that a laugh?

"Do you know who it was you were stealing from?" he asked.

"Yeah. People who wouldn't have missed any of that shit."

"You stole from members of some of the most powerful clans in the country, under my roof. Do you know who the Crescent Moon Clan is?"

I pretended to think. "A bunch of assholes?"

He sighed and thrust a hand into his pocket. His eyes lazily scanned me up and down, and he rubbed his chin. I suddenly felt strangely self-conscious. Frowning, I picked up the white prisoner's uniform top from the end of the cot and pulled it on.

. . .

"I've been given the authority to decide on behalf on my clan, who you offended, what your punishment will be. Do you understand?"

"Sure, I do," I replied gravely. "What will satisfy the clan's call for blood? That's what you're gonna decide. In fact, I bet you've already made up your mind. So why the hell are you here? What do you want from me? You want me to beg? Get down on my knees?"

I chased away the thought of myself getting on my knees in front of him as he undid his belt. Hounds of Hell, what was wrong with me?

"No," he said. "I wanted to see you in person. I didn't want you to just be a faceless mark on a piece of paper when I decide what they're going to do with you."

"Got it. You wanted to see what kind of awesome badass could sneak into your house right under your nose." I spread my arms. "Here I am."

His eyes drifted to my bandaged hand. "That must hurt," he said.

"I've had worse," I said, shrugging. It was a lie.

. . .

"You're missing a pad on that paw when it's shifted. Aren't you?"

How the hell did he know that? I covered my hand self-consciously. "It's a birth defect," I said. "What does it matter to you?"

He shifted his weight from one foot to the other, and for a split-second, I could've sworn I saw his expression soften, becoming the one that belonged to the man on the balcony.

"Nothing important," he said. "You left bloody paw prints across my property. It stood out."

I eyed him. What was he after? He looked like he wanted to say something more about it, like there was more he wanted to ask. What a weirdo.

"What, you want to see it?" I asked. "You have some kind of a paw fetish?"

"What? Don't be ridiculous."

I smirked. From his expression, I could see that I'd managed to get under his skin. It probably wasn't the best idea to jerk the leash of the guy who was going to decide my punishment, but sometimes I just couldn't help myself. And for some stupid reason, I was enjoying screwing around with him. What was hiding under that polished, perfect exterior? What could I say to make that other him that I'd seen come out again?

"They tell me that I can't take this bandage off for at least a week. Apparently, all the running I did really fucked me up."

"You shouldn't have run."

"You wouldn't have caught me if I hadn't stepped on that glass. For an alpha, you're pretty damn slow."

He glared at me with a look that made my heart pound faster. Why the hell was I getting so excited about working him up? It wasn't the same type of pleasure I got from being a smartass to people I hated, this was something completely different.

"Well, congratulations," he said. "You're still the one in the cage. Are you going to tell me your name?"

"Eat dog food."

Christophe nodded to himself, and then took a step forward so that he was right up to the glass. He pressed his palm against it, like he was reaching out to touch me. Part of me wanted to shift and lunge at him, try and give him a little scare, but I knew he wasn't intimidated by me. Maybe that pissed me off a little bit.

"That's fine," he said. "Chief Inspector Burnside is going to get me your name sooner than later, I think it'd be nicer if you could give it to me personally. A proper introduction."

He was right. Eventually, they'd figure out who I was. But it was going to take them a while. As long as I kept my mouth shut, there was nothing on me that could identify me, and the longer they went without knowing, the longer my family could go without this getting to them. Even if it was just a few days, that was fine. Maybe it'd give Jennifer time to think of something to tell Mom.

I leaned forward towards the glass so that our faces were just a few inches apart.

"Eat. My. Asshole."

Smiling to myself, I retreated back to the bed and wrapped myself in the blanket. Playing with him was fun, but I'd had enough. Also, I had a gut feeling that if this kept going, I would eventually let something slip.

. . .

I heard him breath out. "Okay, fine. Goodnight, Eat My Asshole." A moment later, the click of his shoes echoing away and the clang and buzz of the door signaled he was gone. It was my turn to exhale. My heart was hammering.

Christophe Luna.

What the fuck was I feeling?

* * *

The mechanical buzz of the alarm shocked me awake. I had no idea how long I'd been asleep for—it only felt like minutes, if that. The buzz didn't stop, and I sat up, the sleep still clinging to my eyes. I covered my ears to try and drown the sound out, and looked around for a clock. There were no clocks here.

"Wakey, wakey," came the voice of Chief Inspector Burnside as he entered my cell, flanked on either side by two half-shifted police wolves, all muscle and bristling fangs.

"What time is it?" I croaked.

"Time for me to ask you the questions. Get up."

The two officers slapped cuffs on me and muscled me out of the cell. As they hauled me through the compound, I glimpsed morning sunlight coming in through the windows, and caught the time on a wall clock. I guess I'd gotten more sleep than I thought.

They pushed me into a dimly lit room with plain grey walls and one of those two-way mirrors, and slammed me into a metal chair. My stomach gurgled. I was starving.

The chief inspector took the seat across from me. "The only reason why I'm wasting my time with a piece of dog shit like you, is because of who you stole from. Feel lucky. Most trash don't deal directly with the chief inspector. Now, do you have anything you want to tell me? Make this easy for us? Because we're getting what we want, whether it's now, or later."

"Some breakfast would be nice," I said.

"Breakfast, huh? Right. Right, you must be hungry." He pulled out a radio and spoke into it. "Everdeen, they still have breakfast up in the mess?"

"Yes, sir," the radio crackled.

"Bring me a full plate. Everything. Lots of bacon."

. . .

My stomach growled noisily at the mention of bacon, and a few minutes later the room filled with the thick aroma of eggs, sausage, sugary bacon, grilled tomatoes, and beans. The officer handed the plate to Burnside, who placed it on the table just out of my reach. I watched as he picked up a piece of the bacon, and took a bite out of it. It crunched loudly, and he smiled.

"Good shit. I've already eaten, but can always go for more bacon, you know?"

My mouth was watering.

"So," he continued. "What's your name?"

I closed my eyes and thought about Mom and Jennifer. I just needed to hold out. Give her as much time as possible to clean up any evidence she was working with me.

"Jack," I said, eying the plate of food.

"Okay," Burnside replied, with a smug smile. "Good. That wasn't so hard. Your family name, and you can have breakfast."

"Inoff."

. . .

The smile slowly disappeared. "Jack Inoff," he muttered to himself, shaking his head. Then he burst to his feet and swiped the plate off the table. It hit the wall, exploding food everywhere.

"Listen, you little dog shit. I'm missing my kid's race because I have to be here with you, so why don't you just fucking—"

The door opened and an officer peeked his head inside. "Chief."

"What!" he yelled, turning around. The officer flinched, like he was expecting to get a table thrown at him.

"Um, sorry, sir. Uh, he's here again. He wants to see him." He nodded towards me.

"He? What, do you think I can read minds? Who?"

"Mr. Luna."

Burnside groaned. "Hounds of *Hell*. He's here right now?"

"Yes, sir."

. . .

He turned back to me and pointed a fat finger in my face. "*Stay.*"

CHRISTOPHE

Meeting him in person hadn't done anything to settle my mind. I hadn't gotten to look at his paw, and I wondered if I had, if it would've even made any difference. Aside from a handsome face, he was contemptible, obviously unrefined, and completely the opposite of anyone I would've imagined to be my fated mate. Admittedly, I had gotten my hopes up and imagined that maybe something magical would happen and I would discover something amazing.

Irritating. Unrefined. Disrespectful. Just thinking about my interaction with him made my face hot. But what could I expect from a common thief?

And that's all he was. A sneaky raccoon, picking the scraps from the garbage. And yet, I couldn't stop thinking about him.

. . .

I didn't know why I'd decided to come back to the police compound the very next morning. There was no reason for me to waste my time again, but I was compelled to return. I guess, despite everything, I was intrigued. And seeing him was an excuse to get away from regular clan affairs. Meetings, meetings, and more meetings. Taking care of two hungover teenagers. Meetings again.

At least he was interesting.

Chief Inspector Burnside appeared, and I could see he was hiding the fact that he wasn't pleased to see me back again. Still, he put on a smile and extended his hand. The high clans controlled everything, including his salary. He knew he had to play the game.

"Mr. Luna."

"Chief Inspector. Good morning. Any progress with my little intruder?"

"I'm working on it, I promise I'll have something for you shortly. But you know, you don't have to wait for a name to decide on his sentence. You can do that whenever you'd like."

"And I'd like to know who it is I'm punishing," I said. "And I'd like to see him again."

. . .

His smile pulled into a thin line. "Well, that's… I'm questioning him now, and making some good progress. I don't think—"

"I'd like to see him again," I said pleasantly.

The chief inspector's face turned a slight shade of red, and he cleared his throat. "Okay. Sure. Follow me."

"Thank you, Chief Inspector."

He brought me to a small interrogation room with a desk in the center, and Mr. Asshole sat silently behind it, his hands cuffed. The floor was covered in breakfast food. I stepped carefully over a smashed tomato and sat down in the empty chair across from him. The chief inspector crossed his arms and stood by the door.

"Eat My Asshole," I said, and the man looked up at me. I couldn't help but grin.

"What the hell do you want?"

"Just back to talk. Maybe find out what your name is."

He snorted in response.

. . .

"What's all that?" I asked, gesturing to the food on the ground.

"Chief Burnballs here is trying to starve me to death," he said. "I haven't eaten since yesterday."

"Seriously? You must be starving."

"Famished."

I hated the idea of him being hungry, regardless of who he was or what he did, and it angered me that the chief inspector had tried to take advantage of his hunger. It just wasn't right.

"Chief Inspector?" I said.

"Yes?"

"Would you mind leaving us?"

He sputtered a protest, but I cut him off.

. . .

"I insist," I said firmly.

He grunted and turned to leave.

"Oh, and have an officer bring Mr. Asshole here another plate of food, please."

"Now, Mr. Luna, I don't think—"

"No, maybe you didn't. Nobody deserves to be hungry. The food, please."

He stormed off, and a short wait later, an officer returned with a plate of food. I slid it across the table, and he started to wolf everything down.

"Thank you," he said, his mouth bulging with food. It was actually kind of adorable, watching him stuff his face.

"You're welcome, Eat My Asshole."

"Don't call me that," he said as he crunched a piece of bacon.

"Why not? Eat My Asshole is your name, right? What else should I call you?"

. . .

He sighed. "I hate you."

"I Hate You. Strange name."

He ignored me. "Alright, Christophe, what are you doing here?"

"You remembered my name," I said. I was genuinely surprised, and it put an unexpected feeling in my stomach. I didn't give a damn about him, so why the hell was I happy he remembered my name?

"Yeah, well, you're still not getting mine."

"That's fine. Eat My Asshole, I Hate You, I have plenty of things I can call you. I'm fine with them all."

He polished off the rest of the food. "So, what are you doing back here?"

"I want to know what would compel someone to rob the house of a high clan. It's not exactly the low hanging fruit of targets. And yet, even going through all that trouble to learn how to break into my home—and I know it must've been a bit of work, you look like an idiot, but you're obviously very skilled, at least at getting into places—but out of all the things you could've stolen, after choosing such a difficult target, you go for the least important room, with the least valuable things in them. Wallets? The buttons off of a jacket? Those gemstones in the safe were valuable, but I get the feeling that was an afterthought. You didn't originally plan to go for the safe, and that's how you messed up."

He shrugged. "What's that saying? One wolf's scraps are another wolf's banquet? I wasn't looking to get rich, just to take what I needed."

"Oh, how honorable of you," I said. "And stealing was the best way of doing that."

"Yes," he said plainly. "You don't know my struggles."

"Okay, well since an honest job is apparently out of the question, why not just rob the store down the street? Or your next door neighbor?"

"Because," he said, glaring at me. "They're suffering just as much as my family is. You and your fancy friends wouldn't miss any of that stuff. You have plenty more where it all came from. My mom is sick, she can't work. The fucking Blood Gulch Clan sucks away what little honest money we can bring in just for their protection fees. We can barely afford to survive. You have no idea what it's like to live in my world."

. . .

I felt a twinge of anger at hearing him mention the Blood Gulch Clan. They were one of the high clans, but were notorious for dishonorable members and practices. One of their members had put my youngest brother in the hospital, and I despised them.

So, if he was telling the truth, he was stealing to support his family, and taking from the rich because he didn't want to steal from the poor. He was a criminal, and maybe I should've hated him for breaking into my family's home, but oddly, I suddenly didn't feel anymore spite towards him. Now that I knew this about him, I felt for his situation.

If it was true. He could've been lying, but I was certain he was telling the truth. Or did I just want to believe that he was honest, because I thought that we might have…

What?

Some unexplainable bond connecting us from birth?

This was why Father didn't believe in things like fated mates. Belief in things like that weakened resolve. It made for poor leaders. And it made you do stupid things. Stupid, unexplainable, nonsensical, impulsive things.

. . .

"You're right, I don't," I said.

"People like you are always going to fuck over people like me," he said. "Always, and forever."

"Maybe I could help you."

He stared at me, his icy blue eyes narrowing. I could see him trying to figure out what I was after. *I* didn't even know what I was after. How the hell could I help him? Why the hell did I even say that?

"Help me, how? Why would *you* want to help me?"

"Perhaps…I don't want to have you put in jail. Perhaps instead, I'd rather rehabilitate you. Get you work. The Crescent Moon Clan is nothing like the Blood Gulch Clan. We gather our strength through honor and integrity. Through assisting the weak, not preying on them."

He twitched. "Right. And to do that, all I need to do is tell you my name. And then once you have that, you'll conveniently forget about what you just said. All the highborn clans are the same, they only look out for their own."

I gritted my teeth and fought to keep composed. Just the suggestion that my pack was anything like those Blood

Gulch bastards was enough to get my blood boiling. I could've argued, but what would be the point?

And really, why the hell *was* I making an offer to help him?

I stood and straightened my tie. "We aren't all the same," I said. "I imagine I won't be seeing you again. I'll decide your punishment once Chief Burnside has your identity." I turned to leave.

"I'm not weak," he said, barely audible.

"What?"

"I said, I'm not weak."

Is that what that was about? His pride? The smallest smile crossed my lips, but I hid it well. I probably would've done the same in his position.

I left the room, and Chief Burnside was waiting in the hallway.

"We'll take care of it from here," he said, irritably. "No need to come back."

. . .

I ignored him and made my way out of the compound. Stephen was waiting by the car in the garage, and he opened the rear door to let me in. I slid inside. The cool leather seat creaked beneath my weight, its light fragrance surrounding me. Stephen shut the door and the cabin lights slowly brightened. The door to the minibar went transparent, revealing the variety of choice liquors for my drive home. I was back in my world.

The car pulled out of the driveway, and I tapped a button to de-tint the windows so that I could watch the city pass by as we drove out of Wolfheart.

I hadn't really been thinking when I'd made up the offer to give him work. I guess that I'd wanted to prove something to him, to change his obviously jaded mind. Or maybe it was just that I wanted to keep seeing him.

It was absolutely ridiculous. I didn't even know his name. I didn't know a damn thing about him, other than he was a criminal who'd broken into my home. For most sane people, that would've been enough to never want to associate with a person. That would've been plenty of reason to hate someone. But this damn mark, and the possibility that it could be real... It'd gotten a hold of me. He'd gotten a hold of me. I wanted to know more about him.

This feeling made no sense, but it didn't change the fact that it was there, painful and strong. Seeing him in person again had only confirmed it for me. I was attracted to this man. I wanted him.

"Stephen," I said, putting down the divider window between the rear and front seats.

"Yes, sir?"

"I'd like you to get me that man's identity. Full clan assets authorization. Do it quietly and independently of the police."

"I can have it for you by tonight, sir."

"Thank you."

* * *

"Have you arranged for someone to fix that door yet?" Mother asked as we were eating breakfast. "Not to mention the ducts need to be inspected."

"I'm working on it, Mother," I said. "I'll have someone soon."

"It's unsightly," she said. "It's been two days already. Please have it taken care of."

. . .

"And the person responsible for all this?" asked Father. "What did you decide to do?"

"I'm still working on that as well," I replied, as evenly as I could.

"What's taking so long, Christophe? Just dispense with the sentence and be done with it. You needn't take so long on such a small thing."

"It's a man's life, so I wanted to give it due diligence. I'll take care of it after breakfast," I said. "Both things."

He exchanged a look with Mother. I knew what he was thinking—that my idealism wouldn't last forever. Well, I'd hold on to it while I could. Besides, this one was special. Not that they needed to know that.

Mason Arkentooth, twenty years old, omega.

Stephen, using all the resources available to the clan that extended far above the police system, had gotten me his information in just a few hours. After that, I'd gone and done my own research. Mason's story had checked out—he lived with his mother and sixteen-year-old sister. His mother had recently been diagnosed with some unspecified degenerative sickness that'd caused her to lose mobility in her legs. They were barely scraping by, but had still somehow managed to pay off Ackson Bellock's ludicrous clan fees, despite the fact that Mason hadn't been employed in months. Obviously, our place hadn't been Mason's only target.

Had it been up to Father, Mason would be locked up for years and his family thrown to the rabids. I was not going to do that. Regardless of whatever it was I felt towards him, I wasn't going to do that. This was my first leadership act, and I was going to act in the true spirit of the Crescent Moons.

After breakfast, I retreated to an empty sitting room and made a phone call to Chief Inspector Burnside.

"Yes," I said, finally managing a word in between his angry shouting. "No, you heard me correctly, Chief Inspector."

"Listen, we're still working on his identity. I don't understand!"

"Yes, I understand you're still working on identifying him. You don't need to worry about that anymore."

"Mr. Luna, this man *stole* from you. He—"

"Chief Inspector, he's not going to go unpunished. Believe me. I'm simply moving matters into the hands of my clan. So please, don't make me repeat myself. He's to be released immediately, with no further action on your end. Understand?"

There was a moment of angry silence. "Yes."

"Thank you for understanding, Chief Inspector," I said. "The department can always count on a generous donation from the Crescent Moon Clan."

I hung up the phone, and was surprised by a warm, tingling rush that overtook my body. Now I could find out what kind of person Mason really was. I just hoped that I hadn't made the biggest mistake of my life.

MASON

After the police tossed me out onto the street, I hitchhiked a ride across the city to my neighborhood. Normally I would've just shifted and ran, but my stupid paw was still bandaged and healing.

I couldn't believe my luck. It just didn't make any sense—I had no idea why, but for some reason Christophe had decided to let me go. Maybe he was trying to prove something to me, that what he'd said about his clan's honor was true. I didn't know, I didn't care. All that mattered was getting home to make sure that Jennifer and Mom were okay.

I paced around on the sidewalk below the apartment, running through all the different scenarios in my mind. I didn't have any way of letting myself in, and I was too afraid to just knock on the door. I was afraid of what Mom would say when she opened it.

. . .

Finally, I decided to try Jennifer's window. I picked up a bottle cap from the street and tossed it at the glass. After a moment of no response, I scooped up a small pebble and plinked it against the glass. A second later the curtains pulled back and I saw my sister peering down at me. Her eyes widened and she threw open the window.

"Hounds of Hell! Mason!"

I held my finger up my mouth. "Not so loud."

"Where have you been?" she said, lowering her voice.

"Tell you inside. Is Mom okay?"

"She's fine. I said you've been away for work."

"You're amazing. Let me inside."

I went up to the front door, and Jennifer pulled it open. She smiled at me, and I could see she was restraining her excitement to see me.

"Mom, Mason's home."

. . .

"Sorry, I forgot my key," I called.

Mom was in the living room, sitting in her wheelchair watching TV. "How was work, honey? Long shift."

"Yeah," I said. I went over and gave her a kiss on the head. "I'm exhausted. Sorry, Mom, I'm going to go rest."

"Go shower. You stink." She gasped. "And what happened to your hand?"

"Oh, nothing. Just slammed my fingers in a door."

I went to my room and Jennifer followed, closing the door behind her and squeezing me in a tight hug.

"You have no idea how fucking scared I've been," she said. "I've been waiting for the police to turn up. I thought they got you. I saw them…"

"They did. They let me go today. Didn't even figure out my name."

"What the fuck? They let you go?"

. . .

"You won't believe this, but the alpha who chased me? The one that was on the balcony. He's the eldest Luna alpha. He must've decided to have them let me go."

Jennifer frowned. "Why would he do that?"

"The idiot was trying to prove something about his clan. That they aren't all like the Blood Gulch. What a sucker, huh?"

I said this, but my feelings weren't behind my words. I just didn't want Jennifer to catch on to the fact that I was in complete awe of Christophe Luna. I hadn't met many men of integrity. The fact that he'd done that without even knowing who I was…

Some people *were* suckers, but I knew Christophe wasn't.

"I don't get it," she said, "But I guess that doesn't matter. I'm so glad you're okay." She hugged me again, and I saw that she was crying. "I was so scared, Mason. I didn't want you to go to jail. I thought we were done for."

"I'm sorry, Jennifer," I said, hugging her close. "It was all my fault. I shouldn't have made you go for the safe. Especially after all of the precautions we'd taken. I got stupid."

. . .

"You're damn right you did." She pushed away from me. "And I was stupid for listening to you. We have nothing, now. I don't know what we're going to do."

"I'll find work. I'll figure it out, okay? But tell me, did you get rid of everything? All our tools?"

"Don't worry," she said, wiping her face. "It's all gone."

"Good, good. We'll be okay. I'm going to figure shit out. It's back to a legit job for me."

"But, Mason. Legit work won't pay enough. That's why we stole in the first place."

"Hey, I'm trying to be optimistic, here," I said, pushing her shoulder. "You don't have to remind me."

That night, I found myself unable to fall asleep despite the amazing comfort of being back home in my own bed. I'd come so close to the edge, to a fate that would've destroyed my family. I was ashamed of myself, and it wasn't because I'd gotten caught. I should never have taken those risks. Jennifer and I should never have started stealing to begin with.

. . .

But if we hadn't, where would we be now? On the street? Would we have been able to take care of Mom?

Tears welled up in my eyes, and I turned my face into the pillow to silence them.

And I never would've met Christophe. Though that probably wouldn't have been such a bad thing. As much as I was grateful to him, the guy still pissed me off. And as much as he pissed me off, I couldn't deny that I was equally attracted to him.

My right hand started to throb, and I gingerly rested it on the pillow. I couldn't wait to take these damn bandages off. They were starting to itch, and I'd need full use of my body if I was going to find work. Nobody would hire a shifter who couldn't walk on their paw.

Whenever I closed my eyes, I found myself thinking of him, and that pissed me off even more. He was just a pretty face. That was stupidly gorgeous. That I wanted to kiss.

Shit.

I felt like there had to be something wrong with me. The way that he'd made me feel, it just didn't make sense.

. . .

But I'd never see him again. I should've been relieved—he was my judge, jury, and executioner, after all. But I wasn't. I was actually disappointed. I wished that I could see him one more time, and maybe *actually* get to speak to him, to get to know who he was. But that was ridiculous. It'd never happen, and for that I should've been thankful.

* * *

The inside of the fridge was nearly as barren as our bank account. After making a mental note of what we had, I pulled out a mostly empty carton of eggs and a small package of pork belly and set to making breakfast for the three of us. I was in a bind, and needed to start pulling in money soon. Jennifer had been helping Mom get washed up, and she came into the kitchen and leaned against the sink as I cracked the eggs into a pan.

"She's getting worse," Jennifer said quietly. "I think it's spreading further from her legs."

"We'll be fine," I said, not wanting to look at her. I didn't want her to see how scared I was.

"I can drop out of pre-academy," she said. "I can work too."

"No, no. You gotta stay in school, Jennifer. I'll find something."

. . .

I racked my brain, trying to think of options. The problem was that I'd done this so many times before, and always in the end the answer was clear: whatever I was qualified for was not enough to support us. It always circled back to the same option.

I'd gotten my warning. To ignore it would be to condemn myself, for sure. But what else was there…?

"Good morning, you two! That smells wonderful, Mason." Mom wheeled herself to the dining table. "Thank you for cooking." I could see that Jennifer was right, her movements looked even more locked than before.

"No problem, Mom," I said, throwing down the slices of pork belly onto the skillet.

No, I couldn't go back to stealing.

The doorbell rang, and Jennifer went to open it.

"Let me get it," Mom said. "Help your brother with the breakfast." Jennifer started to protest, but Mom put her hand up and wheeled herself over to the front door.

"Get me the plates, Jennifer," I said, turning off the stove.

. . .

"Can I help you?" Mom said at the front door.

"Is this the Arkentooth residence?" came a voice that sent a bolt of electricity through my body.

"Yes?"

"My name is Christophe Luna. I'm here to see Mason Arkentooth."

I turned around slowly and saw that it really was him, standing right there in my doorway. He was dressed the same as I'd seen him every time before—crisp suit and tie, everything polished and fit perfectly. He caught my eye and smiled, and I felt butterflies in my stomach and even more shockingly, a pulse down between my thighs. I nearly knocked the pan off the stove. What the hell was he doing here?

Jennifer looked at me, wide eyed. I shook my head. *We're okay, don't worry.*

I hoped.

"Luna," Mom repeated. "Oh, Hounds! From the Crescent Moon Lunas?"

. . .

"Yes, ma'am."

"Please, come in," she said. "Mason, you know this gentleman?"

"Um, yes," I said, finding my voice. "We, uh…"

"Met through his work," Christophe said. "Security. Isn't that right, Mason?"

"Yeah…" I stammered. How did he know I'd worked in security?

"Maybe you'd like to come in for some breakfast, Mr. Luna?" Mom said.

"Oh, no, thank you. But if you wouldn't mind me borrowing Mason for a moment to talk to him about a job we'd discussed."

"Of course," Mom said, looking delighted. "Mason?"

"Uh, sure. Don't wait up for me, the food will get cold."

. . .

I followed Christophe down the stairs to the street. There was a large black car parked at the sidewalk, and a man opened the rear door for both of us.

"I'm not getting in there," I said, worried that maybe Christophe was here to take me to some secret Crescent Moon Clan prison, that maybe I hadn't actually gotten off the hook. Then again, maybe being locked in his dungeon wouldn't be such a bad thing.

I kicked myself. *No.* This was serious.

"Yes, you are," he said, and he grabbed my shoulder and pushed me towards the car. He may not have been a very fast runner, but he did have an alpha's strength. I thought about shouting, but what good would that do? Nobody would help me. I struggled, and he tightened his grip and shoved the small of my back with his other hand. Again, there was that damn jolt of excitement. *Don't get your hands off me, don't.* It was the first time he'd touched me, and I should not have enjoyed it as much as I did.

I pressed my good hand against the door frame. I could at least make it a little difficult for him. He pushed harder, and I resisted. It felt so wrong, but I was actually getting excited from this. What the hell was wrong with me? This was serious, but I was playing with him...

. . .

"Get *in*," he grunted, shoving me forward. I felt his crotch push up against my ass. *Hounds of Hell!* Either Christophe was just that big, or I could've sworn I felt a little excitement there too. I fell forward onto the leather seat, my face smacking into the cushion. "We're not going anywhere. We're just going to talk."

He sat down and straightened his suit, and I could see his face was slightly red.

"What do you want?" I demanded.

"Is this any way to treat the man who let you out of jail, record free?"

I glared at him, unable to come up with an answer. "How did you find me?"

"The clan has their own resources," he said. "Look, I'm here because I want to help you. I want to offer you some work. A chance to redeem yourself. Get your family on their feet."

"You've already made your point. Your clan is good. Congratulations. I don't need your help."

He gave me a silent, incredulous look. I stared back at him as defiantly as I could, and then deflated.

. . .

"Dammit. I feel like a fucking failure."

He leaned in slightly. "Then let me help you."

"What do you get of this?"

Christophe thought about it, and I saw a brief flicker of hesitation in his confident air. In that moment, I saw the face of the boy on the balcony—searching, yearning… lost? My heart skipped the tiniest beat. What did he want with me?

"I get to confirm something," he said, finally. "And hopefully put something to rest. It's not something I can easily explain."

"I don't get it," I said.

He smiled. "Me neither. So, are you interested in hearing what I have to offer?"

"Tell me."

"As punishment for your robbery attempt, I'm offering you the opportunity to repair the damage you did to my home. The door that was knocked down will be easy, repairing what you did when knocking around inside the air vents might take longer. At the end, I'll have an account set up for your family to help you get back on your feet. How does that sound?"

The stubborn side of me wanted to badly to reject him just because, but I wasn't going to do that to my family. This was exactly what we needed, and I could hardly even believe it was being offered.

"Okay," I said, "Okay, fine. It's not like I have much of a choice, anyway. When do I start?"

He smirked at me. "Well, unless you have something more important to do, you can start right away."

Fifteen minutes later, after notifying Mom and Jennifer about my new job, I was on my way back to the Luna residence—the one place I never would've imagined myself ever returning to. And the craziest, most ridiculous part about the whole thing was that he was in my life again. He sat in the seat adjacent to me, his eyes fixed on the scene flying by outside the car window. I snuck a few glances at him, and couldn't help but smile to myself.

Was it completely insane of me to actually feel excited to be around him?

. . .

"Listen," I said, breaking the silence that had settled between us. "I don't know what you're after, and it's hard for me to believe that this isn't some kind of setup to screw me. But…" I sighed, and forced the words from my mouth. "I want to trust you. Not that I have much of a choice. I guess you know just how bad things are for my family. My mom isn't in the best shape, and with my dad gone, I'm the only one capable of bringing in enough to feed my family. Jennifer, my sister, I can't let her drop out of pre-academy. I made that mistake already." I gritted my teeth. "So, I guess, what I'm trying to say is… Fuck. Thank you. I'm trusting you."

Christophe looked over at me and did something that took me completely by surprise. He put his hand on my knee. "I'm putting my faith in you too, Mason," he said. "And I'm hoping I'm not making a huge mistake."

CHRISTOPHE

Of course, when I'd announced to Mother and Father what I was going to do with Mason, they'd thought I'd gone insane. I told them my justification—that it was in the spirit and duty of our clan, and that this was the type of leader I wanted to be. In the end, it was probably the hate for the Bellocks and the Blood Gulch Clan that won them to my side. I knew they didn't *really* care to help Mason. And in the end, I guess I'd hidden my true intentions for why I was doing this.

Would I have done the same if I hadn't thought that Mason might be special?

I didn't know. And maybe I was a terrible person for that.

The thing was that every second I'd spent with him, even just arguing with him in the police compound, had convinced me that he *was* special, that there was something cosmic connecting us. How else could I explain the way I felt about him? During every bit of those few short moments, my attraction to him had grown stronger and stronger. When I touched him, it was like a jolt of lightning had hit me. I wanted more. I wanted to feel him against me. I wanted to hold him, to take him, to make him mine. Maybe I *had* gone insane.

During that ride home, it took all my strength not to be overwhelmed by his presence. I had to force myself to look out the window so that I didn't stare at him.

And yet, despite all this… He was still a lowborn omega. That was the worst part. We could never be together. Not that there was any explicit rule against it, it just was completely unheard of. Not to mention, Mother and Father would never approve.

What was I expecting from all of this?

I had no idea. But I knew that I needed to do it, or else I'd regret it for the rest of my life.

Mason followed me into the house, and I could see how nervous and uncomfortable he was being back here. I brought him to the coat room, where the old door still hung halfway off its hinges. Inside, the vent cover was hanging open, untouched from when I'd seen him disappear into it.

The only thing that was missing was the climbing rope, which had been taken by the police.

"I probably should've mentioned that I've never done anything like this before," he said, sheepishly.

"You figured out how to break in here undetected through a system of vents, so I think you can probably figure this out. But if you do need anything, let Stephen know. He's the head of our house staff and can supply you with anything."

Right on cue, Stephen appeared, pushing a cart of tools, a replacement door, and electronics.

"Thanks," Mason said. "Guess I'd better get to work, then."

"I'll be back to check on you," I said. I left him there, staring blank faced at the supplies in front of him. I went upstairs, and then ducked behind an outcropping where I could watch him without being seen. He continued to stare the door for a few minutes, occasionally scratching his head, until he finally picked up a drill and started to remove the mangled screws that held the thing to the frame. I sighed. I wanted to find a way to talk to him normally, not with this uncomfortable divide between us. But what chance was there of that happening?

. . .

Father was in his office, and I went to report to him that Mason was here.

"I'm still not happy about this," he grunted without looking up from the stack of paperwork he was poring over. "Having a criminal in our home. He could be taking stock of everything we own."

"I ask that you trust my judgement, Father. I sense that he's a man of good character, just misguided."

"He tried to steal from us. I think that's all that needs to be said. But you've always had a good sense for people, perhaps better than I. I just hope you won't regret this decision."

I do too, I thought to myself.

"Just have him out of here as quickly as possible," Father said.

As I walked down the hallway, Arthur passed by me and looked up from his phone. "Who's the omega?" he asked.

"Mason Arkentooth," I said. "He's the guy that broke in here the other night."

. . .

"The hell is he doing here?" he asked, and I sighed and explained. Arthur gave me a look. "Weird. Okay. Interesting call, Christophe. Maybe I'll go down and introduce myself."

"Don't flirt with him," I said, just a little too quickly. Arthur's eyes narrowed, and a little smile curled on his lips.

"Noooo. Is *that* the reason he's here?"

Dammit.

"I don't know what you mean," I said.

"Hounds of Hell, Christophe. You don't have a crush on the guy who tried to rob us, do you? I knew you were disappointed about the party, but I didn't think you were *that* backed up."

"I'm giving him a chance to redeem himself," I said. "That's it. There's nothing more to this."

Arthur smiled. "It's okay, man. Relax. You don't need to pretend around me, remember?"

I straightened my cuffs and took a moment to recover myself. "Not a word to Mother and Father," I said.

. . .

His smile turned to a laugh, and he clapped me on the shoulder. "I've got your back. But, Christophe, don't let it cloud your judgement."

"It's not," I said, though now I wasn't entirely sure. The way I was feeling about him, the breakneck intensity of it, was like nothing I'd experienced before. What if I had misjudged him? What if I just wanted to trust him?

No.

I couldn't doubt myself. And more importantly, I wasn't going to doubt him.

Arthur's phone chimed, and he feigned an exaggerated sigh and continued on down the hallway. "These girls won't leave me alone…"

As I walked along, I realized that I was smiling. I couldn't believe how good it made me feel to know that Arthur supported me. Having to hold in my feelings, to keep them hidden from everyone… it took a toll on me. It'd been that way my entire life. I was never allowed to be myself, to fully express myself. I was the first alpha, and I always had to act as such. Just having this piece of my own feelings out in the world, finally, it felt so freeing. I walked faster. I wanted to get back downstairs, to check on Mason. I wanted to see him.

. . .

I turned the corner out of the hallway and made my way out to the spot overlooking the coat room, and peered down.

My stomach flipped in shock.

Mason was gone.

"Oh, shit," I said under my breath as I hurried downstairs. The broken coat room door had been taken off of the frame, and I quickly peered inside to see if he was there. He wasn't.

The tools were still scattered on the floor. Stephen. Where was Stephen?

It wasn't so much that I was worried about Mason stealing anything or running away. I knew where he lived. I was worried about being wrong. I was worried that he wasn't the person I sensed he was. That would be worse than anything else.

I took out my phone and dialed Stephen's number. The front door opened and he walked in pushing a cart full of wiring. His phone started to ring in his pocket and he pulled it out, looked at it, and then looked at me. "Sir?"

"Stephen," I said, hanging up. "Where's Mason?" I realized my heart was pounding. *Calm down, Christophe.*

. . .

"He's outside, sir. Making adjustments to the door. I provided him with more tools, I hope that's fine. Shall I retrieve him?"

"No, no, that's fine. Thank you."

I went outside and received the second biggest shock of that day. There he was, Mason Arkentooth, omega, working at a table saw—with no shirt on. The saw whined and kicked up sawdust from the wood panels he was pushing through it. Sweat glistened on the curves of his muscles. I felt my cock pulse to life, and without thinking, I started waving my arms in the air.

"Hey! Hey!" I shouted.

Mason shut the saw off and stared at me from behind a pair of safety goggles.

"What?" he said, irritated. "What do you want?"

"What are you doing?"

"Fixing the fucking door, what does it look like?"

. . .

"But why are you *shirtless*?"

He continued to stare at me like I was an idiot.

"I got hot," he said, flatly. "You've got the damn heating blasting inside there."

"Yes, well…" Now I felt like an idiot, like seeing him shirtless had caused my brain to temporarily malfunction. "It's winter. You… this is… there's a certain standard of dress expected from people employed here…" I was just blabbing.

"I can put my shirt back on," he said.

"No," I replied, quickly. "Don't worry about it." I pointed to his bandaged hand. "Will you be okay?"

"Don't worry. It's healing quickly."

"Okay. Good. Well, if you need any help…"

"Stephen. I know."

"Right." I'd been about to offer my own help. That would've been silly.

. . .

"Okay," he said. After a moment of a staring at each other, he asked, "Is there something else?"

"Carry on," I said, and he turned back to the saw and started it up again. I went back inside, feeling like a fool.

Stephen stood at attention in the foyer. "Everything alright, sir?" he asked.

I rubbed my head. "Stephen? I need a drink."

* * *

I sat in the downstairs study with a laptop and a glass of whiskey, and stared blankly at the spreadsheet on the screen. It was data from the last clan census, but it just looked like a big jumble of numbers to me. I couldn't concentrate. All I could think about was the man working out in the main hall. I could hear the buzz of the power drill as he worked, obviously way more capable than he'd made himself out to be.

After an hour of unproductive staring at my computer screen, I shut the laptop and went to the kitchen to make food. I didn't need to make food, we had top skilled chefs who could do a far better job than I, but I decided that I wanted to make lunch for Mason. I made sure that Arthur wasn't around—I knew he would never stop giving me a hard time if he discovered I was cooking for Mason.

. . .

Each one of us brothers had received some sort of kitchen training during pre-academy, as was customary of a highborn wolf. Surprisingly, Arthur was the best out of all of us, with Loch coming in second, me third, and Vander the least skilled.

I decided to make simple grilled sandwiches, easy to eat while on the job. I had my own special recipe, and I often made them for myself when I was working. I bustled around the kitchen, whipping together everything and putting them on a skillet. Last minute, I decided to make a homemade soup, too. I put everything on a tray, enough for both of us, and brought the food out.

Mason was still shirtless, but now he looked considerably more frazzled and tired. He lugged the new door up and rested it against the frame as sweat dripped down his cheek onto his chest. He frowned and wiped his face with the back of his hand, and leaned to inspect the door frame.

"Shit," he muttered. He let go of the door to get a closer look at a hole cut into the wall where a jumble of wires was exposed. The door teetered and began to fall. He turned and saw it, and dived onto the ground to grab it before it hit the floor. He winced in pain, and I realized that he'd caught it with his injured hand.

. . .

I hurried over and set the tray of food on the ground, and moved the door off of him. "Hounds of Hell," I muttered. "Are you okay?"

He gritted his teeth and nodded. "Fine."

I saw there was a growing spot of red on his bandage. I grabbed his hand. "You're not. You're bleeding."

He tugged his hand away. "I'm *fine*."

"Let me see it," I said, taking his hand again. I took my phone out and called Stephen to bring a first aid kit.

"I told you, I'm fine, dammit."

He tried to pull away again, but my grip was stronger than his and I held him firmly. "You're under my roof, it's my responsibility to keep you safe," I said. "So, shut up. Let me take care of you."

I could see that he wanted to protest, but he shut his mouth and looked away. Stephen arrived with a first aid kit and then quietly disappeared again, leaving us alone. Slowly, I removed the bandage from Mason's hand. It was an old bandage, a bit dirty and now gritted up with sawdust and shavings of metal from working on the door. I put it aside and inspected his bare hand. A deep gash traveled down his palm. It was healing, but catching the door had caused it to partially open again. If this was the paw that matched the mark on my thigh, there was no evidence of it here in human form. I realized my pulse had started to race. I wished I could see his paw and put all of this to rest. But at the same time, I was afraid of what I'd find—and what it'd mean.

"Did you know that bears use their tongues to aid with healing wounds," I said, out of nowhere, and immediately felt stupid. I was nervous, trying to make conversation.

"Good thing we're not bears," he grunted.

I took out some healing salve from the first aid kit and spread it onto his wound. Mason growled and grabbed my wrist, his blue eyes flashing as they met mine.

"Ow, *shit*. You trying to hurt me?"

"Oh, please. Don't cry."

He looked away again. I wished he hadn't. I wanted to keep looking into his eyes.

I took out a fresh bandage and carefully wrapped his hand, making sure to keep it tight. "Done," I said, relinquishing his hand and immediately missing the feel of it in my palm.

"Thanks," he grunted.

"You're welcome. I've, uh, brought lunch, too." I retrieved the tray of soup and sandwiches and brought it over. "Are you hungry?"

"I might be," he said.

"Eat." I put the tray in front of him. "I'm going to help you," I announced.

"With what? The food?"

"Well, I've gotta eat, too," I said. "The food, and the work, too. With your hand like that, I think you need some assistance."

"Stephen can help," he said.

"Stephen has other things I'd like him to do. I'm going to help you. Alright?"

He eyed me, and I thought I saw the vaguest hint of a smile brush across his lips. "I guess I have no choice."

. . .

"Good," I replied. "Now, let's eat. Maybe we can finish getting the door in place before the end of the afternoon."

"Okay," he said. "Have you ever done anything like this? Fixing this kind of stuff?"

"Never," I replied, taking a bite of my sandwich.

For the first time, I heard Mason laugh. I real laugh, non-sarcastic, and it was wonderful. I didn't know I could love the sound of anything so much. I was lost and completely taken. How had this happened to me? I never thought it could be possible, but here it was, it was happening.

"Well," he said. "I guess we're both in the same boat. We'll figure it out together."

MASON

I really didn't need his help, but I would've been lying if I said I didn't enjoy his company. And it still freaked me out how much I enjoyed it. Christophe came from a world that I despised, but spending time around him and getting to know him was starting to make me see things a little differently. Sure, he was snobby and a bit stuck up, but he was also kind and caring, and I could see how much he prided his honor.

He'd chosen to take a chance on me, to trust me and see the best in me. It was more than I probably would've done for myself, if I were in his position.

The attraction I had for him had grown beyond just physical. There'd always been something about him. He carried an intensity about him, a primal and sensual energy buried deep beneath his serious, prim mask that I'd noticed the moment

I'd laid eyes on him. Now I was starting to enjoy getting to know him. Not that I'd ever admit that to him.

"What are you doing?" he growled. "If you put that there, then the system won't arm."

"Oh, you're an expert, now?" I snapped back. "I read the damn instruction manual, the same as you. It says you need to ground the coupling to the electrical system first, otherwise the door won't lock."

"Let me see that. Give that to me." He reached out to grab the piece of the door's security system I held in my hand, and I jerked it away.

"Why don't you go balance your check book, or something," I said.

It was the second day of working on repairing the broken door, and surprisingly, despite arguing about everything, the two of us working together had actually been really helpful. There would've been no way I could've done it by myself, not with my hand the way it was. Christophe could've brought in someone else to help me, but it did make a difference to me that he'd chosen to do it himself, not that he owed me any proof of his integrity.

. . .

"Why did I think this would be a good idea," he muttered. "I could do this myself and I'd already be done."

"Hey, you were the one who almost wanted to screw the door on backwards. I don't think you've done a day of labor in your *life*."

I shouldered him out of the way and lodged the piece into the bracket inside the wall. "There, it's in." I said.

"What do you want to bet that it's not going to work."

"It is going to work."

"I bet you it won't."

"Alright," I said. "If it works, then you have to treat me out to dinner at the fanciest, most exclusive place you know.

"And what if it doesn't? What do I get?"

"Hell if I know. What would you want from me?"

I didn't know if it was just my imagination, but for the briefest moment the look in Christophe's eyes changed. It was a mixture of that look of longing I'd seen him with before, and something else, something that turned my knees weak. It was a dangerous look. A hungry look. Had I just imagined it? Had I only seen what I wanted to see?

"If it doesn't, then… you need to cook dinner for me. At your house."

I cringed. Christophe sitting down and eating dinner with Mom and Jennifer? How embarrassing would that be? The questions I imagined Mom asking Christophe were enough to make me want to shrivel away.

"Cook dinner, okay, sure."

"Shall we turn this thing on? You can change your mind."

"No way. Do it."

Christophe reached for the control panel on the wall, and I held my breath as he touched it. The panel lit up blue, then green, and the word "ARM" appeared on the screen. He tapped it with his finger. There was a whirring sound. Then a click from inside the door. The screen went blank… and then "ARMED" began to flash on it.

. . .

"Fuck yeah!" I shouted, elbowing his arm. "I told you it would work. Told you, told you."

"Alright, alright," he said, shaking his head. "Don't get excited."

I put my hands on my hips. "So. What am I gonna be eating for dinner? Steak covered in gold?"

I couldn't tell if he was just pretending to look annoyed. I could've sworn I saw him betray a little smile as he looked away from me. "I'll figure it out. Tomorrow night. I hope you don't have any other plans."

"Nope. And it better be the fanciest, most exclusive place," I said. "I've got discerning taste, you know."

How had things come to this point? Just a few days ago, the thought of getting along with anyone highborn would've been a complete joke to me, and now I was going to go to dinner with one? It was bizarre to think about. In fact, it was so crazy that it made me want to burst out laughing. The most shocking part about it all was that I was actually happy about it.

After installing the lock system, Christophe disappeared to go take care of what he called "clan business," and I spent the rest of the day putting the final touches on everything before being driven back home by Stephen.

The wail of distant police sirens greeted me as I stepped out from the back of the car onto the gritty sidewalk. In the entrance of my apartment building, that same damn homeless wolf raised his leg and pissed against the wall.

"C'mon, man," I said, stepping around him, and he scowled at me like I'd wronged him somehow. A strained and distant howl pierced the air, followed by an echo of barks and yips. More sirens. Just another evening in the neighborhood.

Inside, Mom was snoozing in front of the TV in her wheelchair. Jennifer was at the kitchen table, doing homework.

"Food's in the fridge," she said, looking up. "How was another day in paradise?"

"Great," I said, and she gave me a look.

"Great?"

I went to the bathroom and removed the bandage from my hand, and then washed up. The wound had healed well. I threw the cloth bandage away, opting for a regular tape one instead. Another couple of days and the wound would be practically gone.

Jennifer appeared in the doorway of the bathroom. "That wasn't the answer I was expecting to hear. Has it really been great?"

I moved past her and went back to the kitchen. Inside the fridge was a plate of spaghetti and meatballs, and I stuck it in the microwave.

"Mom made it," Jennifer said, following me. "Took her forever, but she insisted. So, what's it like there?"

"About what you'd expect. You saw the place. They've got servants to do pretty much everything for them, even wipe their asses."

"Really?"

"Nah. Well, I don't know. If there is, nobody wipes mine for me. But they do have servants doing practically everything."

"So… it's great?"

. . .

The microwave beeped, and I put the plate of food on the table. It smelled wonderful. It made me happy that Mom was still able to cook, even though it must've been really hard for her to do.

"Not the place, I couldn't give two dog shits about the servants and all that. It's… I don't know." I suddenly felt awkward to be discussing this with my baby sister. We could break into houses together, but this was uncharted territory for me. "It's been interesting spending time with Christophe."

"Why?" she asked. She pouring herself a glass of water from the sink and sat down at the table with me.

"I dunno," I said as I stuffed my face with spaghetti. "He's not like what I expected."

"It's pretty weird that he's being so nice to you," she said. "What do you think he's trying to get at?"

"I don't think he's trying to get at anything," I said. "I never thought I'd say this about a highborn, but I think he's…"

Sexy as hell?

"…actually just trying to do the right thing."

. . .

"Hounds of Hell," Jennifer said, smacking her palm against the table. "What if he's got a *crush* on you?"

I coughed, and nearly jettisoned a meatball across the room. "What?!"

"Yeah. What if he fell in love with you, and everything he's done for you so far has been because he loves you? Wouldn't that be so romantic? It'd be just like a story." Then she burst out laughing and pounded her fist against the dinner table. "Except that'd never happen, because nobody would fall in love with your ugly mug."

"Jennifer, don't hit the dinner table," Mom said, half asleep.

"Sorry, Mom."

Mom responded with a loud snore, and Jennifer smirked at me. "Or maybe you've got a crush on him. Do you like him, Mason?"

I shoveled down the rest of my spaghetti and stood up to wash the plate. "Is this the type of stuff that goes through my sister's mind? Aren't you too young to be thinking about that? How old are you, anyway, like twelve?"

. . .

"Uh, I'm only four years younger than you. Hey, where are you going?"

"Another long day tomorrow, gonna knock out." I ruffled Jennifer's hair. "Finish your homework, kiddo."

"Asshole."

"Jennifer, language," Mom snored.

"Sorry, Mom."

I disappeared into my room and shut the door. My heart was hammering. I sat on the bed, and took a few deep breaths. It felt weird and exciting to hear it said out loud. It was true, I *did* have feelings for him. I wanted him.

I stripped down to my underwear and crawled in bed. Every time my mind went to Christophe, my heart started to race. I went over the events of the day, of every interaction we'd had, replaying them in my mind. What had that touch meant? That look? Had they meant something more, or was I just imagining what I desired?

I closed my eyes, and I saw his face. That damn smug smile of his. Those red eyes. The scent of the cologne he wore, and how it mixed with the smell of his sweat when he worked.

He looked so hot when he worked. He'd refused to wear anything but his suit, and I'd given him a hard time about it, but secretly I thought it was sexy as hell.

I felt my cock pulse as it slowly swelled up against the fabric of my underwear. I could feel the omega inside of me aching for him, for the things that only he, an alpha, could do to me.

My thoughts were going to dirty places.

My cock was rock hard, and I released it. I imagined Christophe's, and what it might look like. Strong, powerful, intense, just like him. I imagined how he could take me with it, how he could fill me up.

Hounds of Hell…

I stroked myself, the warmth of my cock filling my fist. A gasp managed to escape my lips, despite my effort to restrain my voice. I bit the back of my hand and kept going.

He could fuck me, if he wanted to. I'd let him. I wanted him to. He could make me his omega, he could hold me down with those strong hands and pound me from behind. He could take me raw, I didn't care. He could let it go inside of me, I wanted to feel his knot, I wanted to feel it all inside of me. He could give me his baby if he wanted.

. . .

Oh, shit…

My toes curled as my cock flexed, and the warmth of my come spilled out over my hand. I gasped for breath and opened my eyes. My cock continued to throb with my climax, and the haze slowly started to clear from my head.

"What was that?" I muttered to myself, reaching for a tissue. I'd never had such wild fantasies fly through my head before.

I fell back into my pillow, my heart still racing. The thrum of a helicopter droned outside the window, and the light from a spotlight momentarily danced across my bedroom floor. I heard wolves yelping.

All I could think about was Christophe. How had things managed to get this deep?

I didn't know. All I did know was that I wanted him. And I wanted him bad.

* * *

The next day as I was riding over to the Luna manor in the back of the limo, Stephen rolled down the dividing window and announced that he would be assisting me with inspecting the ventilation duct system.

. . .

"Where is Christophe?" I asked, trying not to sound disappointed.

"He has other matters to attend to, but has told me to inform you that he has not forgotten about the bet. He will join you for dinner tonight."

"Good." I nodded, though in honesty I had forgotten about the dinner.

Stephen provided a special electronic cable to look at the inside of the ducts, and it was strange to follow the pathway I'd taken to break into the house again. We fed the cable into the system through vent openings in several rooms, and it was my first time seeing more of the Luna mansion.

During all my research checking out the place before the heist, I'd always carried a feeling of distaste for the place, and for every place that I robbed. It was just a place that rich people lived in. Now, as I walked through the massive hallways lined with gigantic, antique oil portraits of regal looking shifters, I couldn't help but feel awed. There was more than just wealth and money behind this place, there was history. I could see that, and even I could appreciate it.

"My family," a voice echoed from down the hall behind me. I turned around, and saw Christophe walking towards us. He gestured up at the portraits. "Their faces are all over this house. Ancestors, going back almost to the beginning of the Luna line. Stephen, I'll take over from here. Thank you."

Stephen nodded, and quietly slipped away.

"I thought you had work to do?" I said. Now I was trying to hide how happy I was to see him.

"I did, but the thought of you wandering around alone… I was convinced you'd break something."

I snorted. "I wasn't alone, Stephen was here. And he's a lot more knowledgeable about this stuff than you are."

Christophe smiled. "So, what are we doing here?"

"I need to show you? You should pay me more."

We continued to work on inspecting the different sections of ducting while Christophe talked about the history of his family, pointing to different portraits and telling me who was depicted.

"So, someday you'll be up on these walls?" I asked.

. . .

"Someday," he said. There it was again, that longing in his voice.

"You don't sound so pleased about that," I said.

He looked at me, surprised. "What?"

"Am I wrong? You sounded unhappy."

"It's my destiny to be the leader of this family," he said, puffing up. "There's no greater honor a son could have. It's everything I've worked for my entire life, what I've been raised to do."

"But…?"

Christophe seemed to be looking somewhere far away. He sighed. "There are times when I wonder if I'm missing something. Like there's still some part of my life that I've yet to find. I don't know if I can be the alpha meant to lead this family without it."

"What is it?" I asked. "What are you missing?"

"I… I don't know," he said. "This is the first time I've ever told anyone this."

. . .

I was unconvinced. He did know, but he just didn't want to tell me. Not that he needed to. It was obviously some very personal stuff. None of my business.

"Destiny, fate… That's all way beyond me," I said. "I have no clue what I'm destined for. Maybe I don't even have a destiny. Maybe that kind of stuff is only for the highborn. I think I'm just here to exist. Maybe my destiny is just to get stepped on by people like you."

"I'm sorry you and your family have suffered because of the highborn clans," he said. "Honorable clans do their best to care for lowborn people, but there's only so much we can do. And not everyone is honorable, though they may claim to be."

I nodded. "I know. I was only half serious. I quickly saw that I was wrong, at least about you. I'm glad you're not like that."

Christophe smiled and squeezed my arm, and I nearly gasped. His touch was electricity to my skin, and all the fantasies I'd had the night before suddenly surged back into my head.

"You have a destiny, Mason," he said. "Everyone does. I believe that."

. . .

We continued along through the house, following the duct's path through the walls, floor, and ceiling, stopping every so often to inspect a new spot. After we ate lunch, Stephen silently reappeared to take over.

"I've got to actually take care of some business now," Christophe said. "I'll be back in the evening to pay off the bet."

"Alright," I said, having to hide the feelings in my voice for the third time. "Oh, I, uh… I know I said I wanted to eat somewhere super fancy, but all I have are these clothes…" I was wearing a t-shirt and a pair of ripped jeans, pretty much the only things I owned. "And I'm kind of dirty from working."

"That's fine," Christophe said. "No one there will mind."

Stephen and I worked mostly in silence, but that was fine with me. I was preoccupied, thinking about Christophe. There was little to no affecting damage in the vents, just some minor dents from Jennifer and my escape, and as the day went on I quickly realized that there wouldn't be much more for me to do. I would be finished paying off my debt, and it looked like I'd be done that very day.

And that meant my time around Christophe was coming to an end.

. . .

For some reason, it hadn't occurred to me that our time together would be so limited. I just hadn't thought about it. This whole thing had happened so quickly, I'd barely had time to catch my breath, let alone make sense of my feelings for him and what would happen in the future.

The answer was obvious—nothing would happen. We'd both return to our worlds. I'd remember his generosity and kindness for the rest of my life, maybe life would get a little better for my family, and I'd need to forget about anything I ever felt for him. It was pointless to hope for anything more than the friendly relationship we had right now. He was a highborn alpha. He had his destiny. And I was nothing. Wouldn't ever be anything.

Hounds of Hell, was I about to cry?

I turned away from Stephen and quickly wiped away a tear. I never cried.

No.

I could never be highborn, but I wasn't going to just be nothing. Christophe said that everyone had a destiny, maybe I just had to claim mine. I had to make something of myself—I didn't know what, but I wasn't just going to scrape by for my family, and I certainly wasn't ever going to go back to stealing.

. . .

I found myself wanting to work slower, or to pretend like I'd found something that needed repair, but it was no use. It was obvious that today would be my last day at the Luna manor, and my last day with Christophe.

Evening hit when I was outside, crouched down on my hands and knees in front of the access panel that Jennifer and I had entered from. I retracted the electronic snake tool from the vent, rolling it back up. Stephen stood over the monitor, and shut it off. I replaced the vent cover and screwed it back on.

"Looks like everything is in order," Stephen said. "And just on time. I'll go fetch master Christophe for you, if you'd like to wait by the front."

"Thanks," I said, glumly.

I followed him around to the front of the house. He went inside, and I waited out by the huge double front doors and watched the sun set over the forest. I tried to brush the dirt off my clothes, but nothing really helped the fact that they were old and frumpy. I suddenly regretted that we were going somewhere fancy. I didn't have a clue how to be fancy. I was going to stick out like a sore paw.

Speaking of sore paws, my right hand had started to throb again, even though it was mostly healed up. I massaged it lightly, hoping that nothing was wrong with it. The front door opened, and Christophe stepped outside. He'd dressed down slightly and no longer wore his usual full suit, just a button up with a cardigan. A special bag was slung around his neck, one that could be worn comfortably as human or wolf.

"Hope I didn't keep you waiting," he said.

Only half the day, I thought. "Nope. Are we going to be shifting?" I asked, gesturing to his bag.

"Yes," he said. "Actually… We aren't going to be going to a restaurant. I hope you don't mind."

"Ah, I see. Probably can't bring someone like me around to places like that, right?"

"No, that's not it at all. You wanted to go somewhere exclusive, so I wanted to take you to the most exclusive spot, with the most exclusive food."

"Where is that?"

"Well, follow me, and you'll see."

. . .

His body trembled slightly, and then transformed. Black fur spread across his skin, and his shape expanded and grew into the powerful form of an alpha wolf. He dropped to all fours as his face stretched into a long muzzle, his ears shifted to the top of his head, and a tail erupted out from above his legs.

"Well?" he said, his voice deep and rumbling, like the engine of a sports car. "I'm going to leave you behind." He turned and started to run towards the forest.

I sprinted after him, my body shifting as I went. I dropped to all fours mid-stride, and quickly caught up to his flank as my wolf transformation completed.

"You're still so slow," I said, and without thinking, affectionately nipped at his hind leg. I cringed inside, realizing the boundary that I'd just jumped, but Christophe only looked over his shoulder at me, his eyes flashing.

We plunged into the forest, racing around fallen logs and trees. I had a sudden flashback to the night we first met—if you could really call it a meeting. More like a tackling.

Christophe was moving fairly slowly and carefully, choosing to maneuver around obstacles rather than leap over them. Then the trees opened up into a trail cutting through the forest, and we crossed onto it, going deeper and deeper. I knew the direction we were going was not going to take us into Wolfheart, so I wondered what Christophe had planned.

. . .

After fifteen minutes of running, we slowed down to a trot. The sun was still setting, but with the cover of the trees, the forest was dark. Then, ahead, I spotted something that shouldn't have been there. Lights. Strings of fairy lights strung up into the branches of a grove of apple trees.

The trail continued straight up to this decorated spot in the forest, illuminated like a garden with hundreds of tiny hanging lights. In the center was a large, flat rock, and on it was a fully set table and two chairs. Christophe trotted over to it and shifted back to human form. He placed the bag down on to the table and unzipped it, and the smell of roasted meat emerged.

"What is this place?" I asked, shifting too.

"The most exclusive place in the world," he said. "Featuring food cooked by the most exclusive chef in the world—me."

I laughed. "Seriously?" I climbed up on the rock and peered into the bag. Inside were two containers of steak and lobster.

"Yes," he said. "Come on, sit."

I sat down, feeling somewhat overwhelmed.

. . .

"I hope you don't mind," he added. "The problem with being a Luna is that everyone knows it. I wanted to get away from that for an evening, and that wouldn't have been possible at a restaurant."

"That's fine," I said.

Christophe removed a bottle of wine and poured out two glasses, and then plated the meals. They smelled amazing.

"This isn't what you were off doing all day, was it?" I asked.

"Partially," he said. "I did actually have clan business to take care of."

"Well, thanks for following through."

We clinked glasses.

"And thanks for giving me this opportunity, Christophe," I said. "I, uh… I'm not really good at expressing myself, but I want you to know that it means a lot to me."

He nodded. "Eat. The food will get cold."

. . .

I dug in, and it was as delicious as it smelled. I couldn't believe that it was something Christophe had made.

"So, what is this place?" I asked. "Besides the most exclusive place in the world."

"It's my little spot of solitude. When I was a kid, it was pretty much the only place I could escape to be by myself. I spent as much time here as I could, which wasn't really much. It was hard to get away. Now, I come here every so often to think or have a meal by myself."

"It's nice," I said, which was the understatement of the year. I'd really wanted to say that it was beautiful, but saying things like that was not really my specialty.

"Stephen notified me that the job is finished," Christophe said.

"Yeah. Thankfully we were pretty careful moving around inside those vents, so there wasn't any damage."

Christophe raised an eyebrow. "We?"

I froze. *Oh, shit.* "Uh… I mean, me. I."

. . .

"You had someone else helping you," he said, laughing. "I had a feeling."

"No, really, I…"

He reached across the table and put his hand on my wrist. Electricity tingled up my arm.

"It's okay, Mason," he said. "I already told you, everything's been forgiven. That includes your partner. But I hope that this won't mean someone is going to convince you to return to this line of work."

I shook my head. "No. No, we're done. Actually, it's my little sister, Jennifer. She's a genius."

"Seriously? I never would've guessed that."

I didn't know why I'd told him, but I trusted him entirely. And I guess I'd wanted him to know that I hadn't been working with someone bad. Or with someone I might've been involved with. Romantically. It was something about the way he'd said "partner," like he thought maybe there was someone secretly waiting for me… Or maybe I was just imagining all of that. I suddenly felt really stupid.

. . .

"Don't worry," he said, squeezing my wrist. "Really, I won't tell anyone. This ends after tonight."

I felt my stomach tighten.

"Yeah. Thanks, Christophe. I guess this is the last day we'll be seeing each other."

We finished eating the rest of the meal in silence. Afterwards, Christophe cleared away the plates and put them into the bag, then refilled our wine glasses. Then he went and turned off the lights. Up above, through the gaps in the tree tops, shone a billion stars. Christophe took his glass and lay down on the edge of the rock, throwing his hands behind his head to make a pillow as he gazed up at the sky. It was the first time I'd seen him look so relaxed, so casual. It was like seeing a totally different person. I took my glass and joined him.

"I can't see this kind of view from where I live," I said. "Too many lights. There's so many stars up."

Christophe nodded silently. In the continued quiet that'd fallen between us, my heart started to pulse faster. I could hear it thudding in my ears.

"Maybe," he said softly, "This doesn't have to be the last day we see one another."

. . .

My heart jumped, and I looked over at him. "Huh?" I thought I'd misheard him.

Christophe continued to stare up at the stars. Then he slowly turned to look at me, his crimson eyes glimmering in the dim light like molten stars. I could feel my pulse throbbing in the palm of my right hand. It didn't hurt, but it felt hot, and strange.

"Mason, I don't want this to be the last day we spend together."

I jumped when I felt his fingers touch my hand, then slowly wrap around it. The pounding I felt suddenly vanished, leaving my hand tingling, like it'd fallen asleep. *Was this actually happening?*

"What do you mean?" I stammered. I felt frozen in place.

Christophe leaned in. I closed my eyes.

Then I felt him. Softness and warmth against my lips, the tingle of his breath against my cheek.

I nearly punched him in the face in surprise. Instead, thankfully, I kissed him back. My lips melted into his, and I felt the world begin to swirl and give way, like we were the only two people in existence. Our kiss started with just small tastes, and slowly grew stronger and hungrier. We both seemed to not want to be the first to stop. I felt Christophe's tongue tease against my lips, and I welcomed him inside, greeting him with a flick of my own tongue.

Our tongues continued to trade back and forth, and gradually our kisses became smaller and lighter until I was left breathless, my lips parted and waiting for more from him. An ache pulsed between my legs.

"What is going on?" I whispered in a daze.

"I thought it might be obvious," he said. "That I felt this way for you."

"Not to me."

"Not even the romantic dinner?"

"This was romantic?"

He smirked. "I thought *I* was clueless."

. . .

"Shut up." I kissed him again, and grinned. "Wow." Still in disbelief, I planted a few more pecks on his lips, and laughed. "This is insane. This doesn't feel real."

"It doesn't," Christophe agreed. "Especially because I thought you hated me."

"I mean, I kinda did. But to be honest… Oh, this is fucking embarrassing to say."

"Tell me."

I hesitated for a moment. "I was attracted to you from the moment I set eyes on you. I'd never been drawn to anyone like that before."

"When I came to the police compound?"

I shook my head. "No," I said. "Even before that. It was the night I broke in. Jennifer and I were scoping out the house from the forest, and I saw you come outside on the balcony. That was the first time I saw you. I remember you looked like you didn't want to be there. Like there something that was bothering you. It's crazy how vivid that memory is in my mind."

. . .

Christophe's gaze turned back to the stars. After a moment, he asked, "Mason, would you be willing to believe that there's such a thing as destiny if I could prove it to you?"

"How could you prove destiny?"

"When I was a little boy, my father took me to see the clan Teller to have my destiny read. My father always would tell me that it was a bunch of dog shit, but it was part of clan tradition and so I had to go. But what the Teller told me has stuck with me my entire life. Secretly, I've always wanted to believe that what he said would come true."

"What did he say?"

I watched Christophe's face and saw the waves of emotion that crossed over it as he stared up into space. His hand, still holding mine, started to tremble slightly. "He told me I'd one day meet someone who was destined to be my mate. He said that a birthmark I carried on my body would match the paw of that person. The truth is that I've been drawn to you from the very beginning, too. And that I think—no—I *feel* that there's something connecting us. And I think that's what you felt, too."

Suddenly, I remembered Christophe asking me about my paw back when I was being held in jail. He'd asked about my missing paw pad.

. . .

"And you think that my paw is the one that will match you?"

And what if it's not?

Christophe seemed to read my mind. "It's true that I pursued you because of what I saw on the ground on that night. But now I know that whether it is or isn't, it doesn't matter. The pull that I felt towards you was real. I believe that the paw mark I saw that night was the one that belonged to my fated mate. I don't need to confirm it. I already know it, now more than ever."

My head spun. *Fated mate*. And yet, as much as it was to take in, I felt a lightness, a clarity, like it all made sense. That was the reason for why I felt this way. What else could explain such a powerful and sudden feeling? What else could explain why it felt so damn perfect?

I rolled over onto Christophe, cutting his view of the stars off with my eyes. Then I kissed him again. It was amazing how easy and natural it felt to kiss him. As easy as breathing. I stroked his cheek with my right hand, and then rested on his chest. Then I closed my eyes and concentrated on shifting only my hand.

"I want to know," I said. "Let's see how full of shit Tellers are."

. . .

He laughed, but I could tell he was nervous. Christophe believed in all of that, after all. And maybe I wanted to, too. But I wasn't holding my breath.

"Are you sure?" he asked.

"Damn sure. If you are."

His expression changed as he steeled himself, and he sat up, guiding me back by my shoulders. "If you don't mind," he said, and I moved off of him. Where was this birthmark?

His hands went down to his belt, and a huge lump rose in my throat as he unbuckled it and unzipped his fly. I felt my cock throbbing with my heartbeat, and it pushed firmly against my underwear. I shifted myself slightly, hoping he wouldn't notice the rising bulge in my pants.

Christophe opened his pants and untucked his shirt. Then he slowly slid his trousers down his thighs, and off his ankles. He folded them neatly and placed them down next to him on the rock. I immediately saw it, and my heart skipped a beat. On his right inner thigh was a dark mark that on first glance I could've easily mistaken for a tattoo. It was clear—a paw print with a missing pad.

. . .

Suddenly, my paw began to tingle and throb slightly. I kneeled down in front of him, and then slowly reached out my paw and pressed it again his mark.

The tingling feeling spread through my paw, and Christophe gasped, his eyes widening.

"What?" I asked. "Do you feel something?"

"No, your paw's just cold," he said, and I laughed.

"It matches," I said. "I can feel it. It really matches."

He nodded. "I can feel it too." Then he slid his hand around the back of my neck and pulled me into a kiss.

I shifted my paw back to my hand, and my palm filled with the warmth of his thigh. Then I felt a firm press against my wrist. I looked down, and saw it was the tented bulge of his excitement. He looked into my eyes, and I kissed him as I let my hand wander.

Christophe sighed as I made contact, and I explored the shape of him with my palm and my fingertips. I caressed his bulge as my heart hammered in my chest, driving blood down to my own aching erection. I slipped my fingers beneath the waistband of his underwear, and slowly pulled it down to reveal him.

Oh, shit!

He was huge. Alpha sized. Perfect. With the light of the stars above us, I only wished I could see him better.

I wrapped my fingers around him. Christophe's cock, in my hand, right now. I didn't care how fast this night was going. In my entire life, I'd never felt anything as right as what was happening between me and Christophe right now.

He was so hard, practically throbbing in my grasp. Suddenly, a brisk wind blew through the forest, rustling the branches of the trees. Soft clouds of vapor curled from our mouths with each breath.

"Are you cold?" It felt like a silly thing to ask with how hot his cock felt in my hand. He shook his head.

"Are you?"

"No."

. . .

I started to stroke him, and he tossed his head back and groaned. He pulsed lively in my grip, and his head glistened with precome. I lowered my head down to him and teased him, flicking my tongue across his tip. Then I traced one of his veins down his shaft until I reached his balls, and lightly danced my tongue across the soft skin of his sack. He shuddered and moaned, and I felt him pulse in my grip. He looked down at me, and I smiled back up at him, happy to be getting this reaction from him. Then I opened my mouth, and a hot cloud of vapor puffed from my lips as I enveloped him.

His girth filled my mouth, and I did my best to suck him down to the hilt. He was delicious. Amazingly delicious. I couldn't get enough of him. I bobbed and sucked, gulped and gagged. My cock was aching for touch, so I drove my hand down into my pants and started to touch myself out of desperation. Christophe saw. He pushed me off of his cock and drew me into a rough kiss before flipping me onto all fours, my ass facing his face. Hounds of Hell, I hadn't realized how strong he was.

He yanked at my pants and I fumbled to help him get them off. Soon they and my underwear were around my ankles, and I kicked them aside into the dirt. My cock hung above his face, so hard and hot I could've sworn it was giving off its own steamy vapor. I watched as he slid his hands up my thighs and around my ass cheeks, and slowly pulled my hips down, down, down.

I moaned as my cock made contact, pushing past his soft lips into his warm mouth. I turned my attention back to his dick, sucking him as he sucked me. I was wild for him. Feral. I'd never felt such a crazy hunger, and not just to taste him but to *have* him. I wanted that thick cock of his in more than just my mouth.

I took him deep, coating his cock with my saliva as his tongue played up my shaft and danced across my asshole. I murmured against him, my moans gagged by his girth.

"What did you say?" he growled. His voice had changed again. It was the hard, commanding voice of an alpha.

"I want you," I said. "Christophe, I want you."

He pushed me off of him. I crawled on all fours, my knees scraping on the rock. I didn't care. Christophe came forward, and I caught a glimpse of the mark on his thigh. My paw mark.

Fated mates.

We were destined for each other. Marked from birth.

The thought was insane. Absolutely crazy. But I didn't care. Everything had changed for me. I was swimming in my want for Christophe, and I knew that it all was true. Nothing could've changed my mind about that now.

. . .

I turned around and presented myself to him. Out in the forest on this rock table, I felt almost like a sacrifice. I liked that thought.

Everyone has a destiny.

They just had to grab it. Here was mine, and I wanted to surrender to it.

Christophe came forward, and brought his face down to my ass. I could feel his hot breath on my skin. "Why don't you tell me your name?" he said.

"Huh?" What the hell was he talking about? I was aching for him, dying for him to be inside me. "Mason," I said.

"Are you sure?" He grinned at me. "I thought it was…"

He swirled his tongue across my opening, and a shiver of pleasure ran through my body.

"So, what's your name, again?"

"E-eat my asshole," I said, almost begging.

. . .

Christophe answered with his tongue, and I replied with a moan. Soon, I couldn't take it anymore. "Fuck me," I said, now actually begging. "Stop teasing me."

He straightened up, and I felt his cock press against me as he leaned over me. I looked back over my shoulder to meet him, and kissed him. Then he gripped my waist with one hand, grasped himself with the other, and pushed forward to my entrance. I realized that I was wet for him there. It was the first time I'd ever experienced that, an omega's excitement.

Take me…

The words crossed through my mind, and then fell from my lips. I cried out as Christophe entered me. His cock spread me open, pushing all the way to the hilt in one go. He didn't take his time or go slowly. He pumped in hard, his abs slapping hard against my ass as he fucked me. As proper and reserved as Christophe had always been, he was like a different animal now. And as much as I'd have liked to fight against him before, now all I wanted was to surrender to his cock.

Our moans and the sounds of us filled the quiet forest, and I wouldn't have been surprised if our voices carried all the way back to the Luna house. Christophe pushed his hand against the back of my neck, pushing my face down against the cold, smooth rock. He pounded his cock into me, the swell of his head making waves against my most sensitive spots. I didn't even need to pleasure myself. His cock was doing all the work, and I was getting thrown towards the edge.

"You're going to make me come," I gasped. "Fuck, Christophe, oh, *fuck!*"

He answered by pounding in harder and deeper. I looked back at him, wanting to see him when I came. He gazed back at me, his teeth gritted as puffs of vapor escaped with every ragged breath. He squeezed me harder and slammed in one final time as he let out a long and satisfied groan. I felt his cock throbbing inside of me as he came, filling me up with his knot. My eyes fluttered back as I was driven to my climax. The stars whirled above and then popped and exploded in my head as I came. The orgasm felt endless, like I was locked in pleasure just as his cock was locked inside of me, held by his knot as he spilled himself into me.

And then slowly, things came back into focus.

Silence returned to the forest, accented only by our rapid breaths. Christophe slowly pulled out of me, and I collapsed onto the rock. My legs had turned to jelly from the intensity of it all, I could barely move. Christophe lay next to me, and wrapped me in his arms.

"Hounds of Hell," I managed. "Christophe, that was insane. That was insane."

. . .

"I know," he said. He sounded a little shocked. "That was incredible."

I found my pants, and we both got dressed and cleaned up the best we could. He turned the fairy lights back on and examined my face for the first time in the light. I held him tightly, mostly because I just didn't want to let him go, but also because it was a lot colder than I'd realized. He took my face in his hands and kissed me.

"This was more than I could've hoped for," he said.

I found my hand wandering down to his thigh, where the mark was. "This is real," I said, still in disbelief.

"This is real," he said, and kissed me again.

The primal intensity of the moment was fading, but the yearning for him was still there, like an afterglow. My head spun. I didn't know it was possible for feelings for someone to get that strong so quickly. The reality of the situation was starting to dawn on me.

"Christophe…"

. . .

"Yes, Mason?"

"Are we going to be okay?"

I was still me, he was still him. We still belonged to different worlds. Would a fated mark change that? We knew the mark was real, but would anyone else? Would anyone care?

"Yes," he said. "Of course. This can be our place. Our secret place. We'll make things work. I'll find a way."

I wasn't sure what to make of that answer. Could fated mates really stay hidden? Was that something that could be a secret?

I had to trust that this would work. After all, hadn't fate brought us together? The mark proved it, right? I had to believe that was true, because I was in too deep. I hugged him close. I didn't want him to see my doubt.

CHRISTOPHE

Father did a quick inspection of the coat room door, looking neither impressed nor unimpressed.

"And the air system has been repaired as well?"

"Yes, Father," I said.

"So, we're going to be paying this man?"

"Mason Arkentooth, yes."

"Remind me again, why are we paying the criminal who caused all this damage to repair it?"

. . .

I hoped that Father hadn't seen my left eyelid twitch in reaction to what he'd just said. It'd been three days since Mason and I discovered our feelings for one another, and we'd met every evening at my—now our—secret spot in the border forest. It angered me to think about what Father's image of Mason was—an untrustworthy, uncouth, lowborn criminal. I knew, because that was what I'd seen him as too, but it became so clear so quickly that that wasn't him. I understood the reasons for why he'd turned to crime, and I'd fallen for him because of it.

Father was wrong. Fated mate marks *were* real, and I'd found him. After holding on to that possibility for my entire life, I'd actually found him.

"Mason and his family have been taken advantage of by the Blood Gulch Clan, as I'm sure many other families just like them have. He's not a bad person, just someone doing whatever he could to protect and provide for his family. I wanted to give him an out from that path. And I wanted to prove that not all the highborn clans are like that."

"Right, right," Father said. "You did well. Though, I don't quite understand why you had to personally help him. It becomes troublesome to personally involve yourself in every bit of business you do. Part of being a good leader is knowing how to prioritize."

"I know that, Father," I said. "And I wanted to prioritize Mason."

. . .

Father gave me a questioning look, and then shrugged. "That's your prerogative, I suppose."

That night, I went out to the forest spot early to set the place up for our meeting—blankets, pillows, a portable heater, and several bottles of wine. In order to keep this a secret, we couldn't meet anywhere else, but I was fine with that. Coming out to a hidden place in the forest to meet Mason was exciting and romantic. Every moment was a thrill.

I opened a bottle of wine and laid out on the rock, which I'd draped with furs and blankets, and stared up at the dusk sky. I felt free and light, like nothing could touch me. When was the last time I'd felt this way? I couldn't remember. It had to have been when I was just a teenager, but I couldn't be sure. Maybe I'd never felt this light before. It was like for the first time in my life I wasn't stressing about the future. All I wanted was to be here with him.

An hour passed, and the sun had gone down. I switched on the fairy lights and the heater, and finished a third glass of wine.

Mason was late.

I checked my phone, but there was nothing. That should've been reassuring—we'd agreed to avoid contacting each other by phone unless it was an emergency—but I still couldn't help but be worried.

Another hour passed. I fingered my phone in my pocket as I wondered how long would be appropriate before I called him. I shifted to my wolf form and sat up on the rock, my nose lifted to the breeze.

After thirty minutes, I caught Mason's scent, and fifteen minutes after that, I heard him running through the forest. I shifted back to human form as he emerged out of the trees. He shifted to human form too, and wrapped me up in a tight hug.

"You're late," I said.

"Don't tell me you were worried about me," he said.

"No," I said. "If you hadn't come, I would've just enjoyed this bottle of Lupanian red by myself. Would've been a nice time."

"Shut up," he said, and kissed me. "Sorry I'm late."

"Is everything alright?"

. . .

There was a pause before he replied, "Yeah, everything's fine."

I held his shoulders and looked him in the eyes, and he looked back at me with a stubborn fierceness. I could tell he was hiding something.

"What is it?" I asked.

He sighed and sat down on the fur spread. "This is nice. Warm."

"I figured we ought to make the place a little more comfortable," I said, and poured him a glass of wine. "Considering we use it as both a table and a bed. So, what's going on?"

He graciously took the wine from me and took a long sip. "It's really nothing. Just, my mom's condition is getting worse. She was struggling just to move her wheelchair around today. Jennifer and I had to help her."

"The healers don't know what's wrong with her?" I asked.

"We've only been able to afford to take her to a small clinic. They weren't trained or equipped to diagnose her."

. . .

"Hounds of Hell, Mason. I can arrange to get her care."

He smiled sadly. "Thanks, Christophe. You've already done enough, I don't deserve any more help. I don't want to take advantage of your kindness."

"Don't be ridiculous, Mason," I said. "You aren't taking advantage of anyone. You're my fated mate, Mason."

I wrapped my arms around him, and he hugged me tightly.

"How long, Christophe?"

"How long?"

"Could you secretly take care of my family? It's not a big deal now, but how long could it last? I couldn't expect that of you. And you know you couldn't do it."

I frowned. "What do you mean?"

"I wish I wasn't lowborn," he said, and he touched my thigh where the mark was. "This made me believe that there's actually magic in this world. Real magic. But how can we be fated mates when we can't even be together?"

. . .

"We *are* together," I said. "Right here. Right now."

"Yeah, but will we always meet here, like this?"

"This is our paradise. We can escape from both of our worlds here."

He laughed. "For how damn smart you are, you can be kind of naïve about stuff sometimes, Christophe."

"I'm not naïve. I want to be with you, Mason. With you, I've finally found real happiness in my life. I no longer feel like I'm missing something. And once I take over the clan, we don't have to worry about anything. I'll be able to change things. We won't have to do it like this anymore."

"And until then, we've gotta keep meeting in the middle of the woods," he said.

"Yes," I said. "And I'd keep doing it forever if it was the only way we could be together."

"I don't want to be a secret," Mason said. "I don't want to be your secret."

. . .

My heart dropped."I wish we didn't have to be a secret. But I don't know what other choice we have."

Mason nodded sadly. "Right. I know." He wrapped his arms around my waist and hugged me, burying his face into my neck. "Sorry, Christophe," he murmured. "There's just been a lot going on."

"Don't apologize," I said, and kissed him on his head. He was right. I'd gotten so caught up in the moment of this thing that had grown between us that I hadn't stopped to give any thought to what Mason was going through. It was selfish of me, expecting that this could be our normal. Selfish, and it *was* naïve.

I'd constructed this idea that this would be our secret to share, but Mason felt like he was *my* secret. And he was right, as terrible as it was. This had to be a secret because of my family, not his.

Mason kissed my neck as his hands moved across my jacket, tugging it lightly. I shrugged it off my shoulders as his lips made their way up to my ear, where he nipped my earlobe and sent a shiver coursing through my body down to my cock. I pulled his shirt off and pushed him back onto the furs, planting hungry kisses all along his chest. He moaned as I brushed my lips against his nipples, and when I brought my hand down between his thighs I felt his excitement waiting for me.

. . .

I wanted this to be forever. Every day I spent getting to know Mason was bliss. I'd never felt so comfortable with another person in my entire life.

How could I make this right? What could I do for the man who I knew was my fated mate? For us?

I continued to make my way down his chest, kissing across the landscape of his abs until I reached the top of his pants. I unbuttoned them, and slowly drew down his zipper, one tooth at a time. He looked down at me, eagerly waiting for my touch, and I gave it to him. I pulled his pants down his thighs and pressed my lips against the tall bulge of his underwear, kissing and caressing his cock through the fabric.

"Stop teasing me," he growled. "Or I'll beat you up."

I smiled at him and slipped my fingers beneath the waistband of his underwear, and then pulled them down. His cock stood tall and thick, and I drew my lips over the tip to sample it. His gorgeous blue eyes looked down at me as I slowly lowered myself down, taking him inside of my mouth. I went slowly, savoring both his flavor and his little twitches of pleasure.

Nothing in the clan rules said that a lowborn couldn't be mated to one of us, it was just frowned upon, especially for a first alpha. But there was no rule against it.

. . .

What was I willing to sacrifice for Mason? Was I willing to lose everything? My destiny?

For nearly my entire life I'd believed my destiny was to lead the clan. It was what I'd been raised to believe. But…

Mason moaned and thrust his fingers through my hair as I took him deep into my throat. I wrapped my fingers around the base of his shaft, gripping his thickness tightly as I massaged his balls with my other hand. When I pulled off of him, a thick line of saliva dripped from my tongue to the glistening tip of his cock. I gasped to catch my breath, and then dove back in.

But what if I had a different destiny?

I still remembered what the Teller had told me, over twenty years ago. He told me I would become a loyal wolf, who would rise when the occasion called for protecting what I held most dear. I'd always believed he was talking about leading the Crescent Moon Clan. But maybe that wasn't it at all. Maybe that wasn't my destiny?

What if my destiny was…

"Fuck me, Christophe," Mason said, his voice low. "I want you to fuck me, right now."

. . .

He pulled his knees back to his shoulders, opening his legs up to me. I grabbed a pillow and pushed it underneath his ass, then ducked down, grabbed his cock, and ran my tongue all the way from his entrance, up his balls and to the tip. I stripped off my trousers and brought my erection up to his waiting hole, and slowly pushed inside.

I couldn't stop myself from moaning as Mason's tight warmth enveloped me. He threw his arms around my neck as I began to rock my hips, thrusting deep into him.

"Ah, fuck, Christophe," he groaned into my ear. "Don't stop."

His voice made me even harder, and I fucked him deeper, pushing his legs back by his ankles as far as they would go. He was so tight, it felt like he was holding onto me, begging me not to pull out of him.

I was fighting to hold on, but I knew I couldn't for long. It was like were perfectly made for each other, and every movement of my hips, every thrust and pull, was pure ecstasy. I kissed him, putting everything I felt for him into it as I drove all the way in to the hilt. I was coming to the edge.

"I'm going to come," I said.

"Me too," he cried. "Wait for me. Wait for me."

. . .

I bit my lip and squeezed his thighs, doing everything I could to stop the climax.

Mason grabbed at the furs, balling them up in his fists as he moaned. "Oh, *fuck!*"

His cock flexed, and I felt him tighten around me. I was powerless. The orgasm struck me and wouldn't let go. I slammed in as deep as I could, pouring myself into him as his cock throbbed out thick lines of his finish up across my chest.

I pulled out of him, my head spinning with stars. I collapsed next to Mason, and he wrapped me up in his arms. "One more thing," he murmured, and licked his own come from my chest.

We curled up together in the bundle of furs and blankets, the warmth from the heater radiating over us.

"Perfect," Mason whispered, his face pressed into my neck. "So fucking perfect."

I kissed his head and hugged him close.

What if...

. . .

My destiny is...

To be with him?

* * *

I paced nervously around the smoking room. My palms were sweating. It was unlike me to lose my composition so easily, but this wasn't any ordinary meeting. Maybe I should've picked a different place to ask Mother and Father to talk. I hadn't felt this way since I was a child, but all the portraits of my ancestors were starting to feel like they were judging me, like they were all glaring down in disapproval. If Father approved, that was all that mattered. His word was the clan word. But getting his approval was the difficult part.

What are you willing to sacrifice?

I took a deep breath, and found myself going for the tumbler of brandy on the liquor table. I stopped myself. I didn't need it. I straightened as I heard the door open behind me, but when I turned around it wasn't who I'd expected.

"Oh, hey, Christophe," Arthur said as he walked into the room.

"Arthur, what are you doing in here?" I asked.

. . .

"Uh, I live here, too. Pretty sure I'm allowed in here." He went over to a bookshelf and scanned the books.

"I'm sorry," I said, shaking my head. "I didn't mean it that way. I'm just a little jittery right now."

He picked a book from the shelf and tucked it under his arm. "Everything alright?"

I sighed. "No. Not really."

"Oh. What's going on?"

"This is going to seem like it's from out of nowhere, but… Mason and I are together."

His eyes widened. "No shit? Hounds of Hell, Christophe. I didn't expect that you two would *actually*… Damn. A secret, I guess? Don't worry, I'll keep it to myself."

"Arthur, did you ever When you were young, did Father ever take you to the Teller? I don't recall."

"Sure. I think all of us saw the Teller, right? Clan tradition."

. . .

"What did he tell you?"

"I don't know. Something about having a righteous heart, and making a sacrifice. Blah blah, just a bunch of dog shit, I guess. Why? What did he tell you?"

"You know the birthmark I have on my thigh?"

Arthur nodded. "Sure. Muddy paw print."

"He told me that it was something called a fated mate mark. That it actually showed the paw mark of the person I was fated to fall in love with."

"Okay," Arthur laughed. "Yeah, so we've confirmed he was full of a bunch of dog shit." He stopped laughing when he saw my expression. "Right?"

"I don't know. Father told me it was nonsense, too. I guess I believed that. But… You're not going to believe this, Arthur, but Mason's paw matches the mark."

"Oh, come on, Christophe. Van I could see buying into that, but not you."

. . .

I shook my head. "I'm positive, Arthur. It's true. And I know the way I feel about Mason."

He studied me for a moment, and I could see that he understood how serious I was. He stroked his hair back, and exhaled a long breath. "Wow. Okay. So, what are you going to do?"

At that moment, the door to the smoking room opened again, and Mother and Father walked in. Arthur looked me, his eyes wide with realization. "Good luck," he muttered, and slipped away.

"What is it you need, Christophe?" Mother asked.

"You know it's unnecessary to get our permission on official matters," said Father. "I trust your judgment."

My palms were sweating again, and my heart was racing. "This is a matter that still requires your approval."

He and Mother exchanged a glance. "Go on."

"I don't know how to deliver this, so I feel I should just tell you outright. When I was five, you took me to see the clan Teller, and he told me the meaning of the mark on my leg. He said it was a fated mate mark, and that it would bind me to the person who I was meant to be mated to."

"Yes," Father said. "I remember."

"I've found the person who matches my mark."

They exchanged another glance, and Father spoke. "Christophe, the Teller's words are only meant to form a structure on which to begin your life. They don't actually see the future."

"That's not entirely true, Basch," Mother said, to my surprise. "The Teller told me I would have four sons, and that one would be an omega. And…"

Father snorted. "It's nonsense," he said, "And you should know it more than anyone else, Stella. Who is this person?"

I took a breath. "Mason Arkentooth."

"Hounds of Hell," Father said, his voice a low rumble. "You can't be serious."

"Mother, Father, you know me. You know that I'm not one to make rash decisions."

. . .

"Christophe, he's a *criminal*!" Mother said. "He's a lowborn criminal."

"No, Mother," I said. "He's a good man. He's strong, smart, and loyal. His situation is not his fault."

"He made the decision to become a thief," Father said. "That doesn't strike me as very honorable."

"You don't know him," I said.

"And you do? You've only just met him!"

"The mark, Father. I wasn't sure I believed it, but how else can I explain the connection I feel with him? That I've always felt to him?"

"So, this is why you wanted to help him…"

"No, I was honest when I told you my reasons. I decided on that before I fell in love with him."

Mother covered her mouth, and the look on Father's face just about broke my heart. I'd never seen him look so disappointed in me before.

What are you willing to sacrifice? Everything.

I had to be. If I really believed in what I felt for Mason, if I truly believed in the prophecy of the fated mate mark, then I had to be willing to give it all up.

"We can't approve of this," Father said. "I'm sorry, Christophe. You mustn't see him."

"Father, after all the thought I've given this, I know that this is my destiny."

"Your destiny is to lead this family."

"With Mason by my side," I said. "Without him, I'll be incomplete forever. I'll never be able to be the leader you think I'm meant to be."

"Don't be *ridiculous*," Father boomed. "You do your duty to your family!"

I didn't budge, but I could feel tears coming to my eyes. "You know how much the clan means to me. But how can I deny love and fate? If I sacrificed it all for one person, then I hope you'd be able to understand just how I feel about them."

"Christophe, this makes no sense." Mother said. "What are you saying? Basch, stop him!"

I turned to leave. My Father only stood and watched, his face pale with shock.

I hurried downstairs, shifting as I went. Arthur appeared from somewhere, falling into step beside me.

"What happened?" he asked.

I couldn't bring myself to look at him. "I have to leave," I said. "I need to figure this all out."

"Leave? You can't be serious. Hey! Christophe!"

I dropped to all fours and threw open the front door.

"Don't be insane!" he shouted after me. "Don't forget who you are!"

. . .

I knew who I was. In fact, I knew myself better than I ever had before. For nearly my entire life, I'd felt like I was missing a piece of who I was. That deep down, I knew that what I'd come to believe was my destiny was only a part of the picture. I'd been searching a long time to find that missing piece, and now I'd finally found it in Mason. I was not going to let him go.

I ran. I didn't care how far he was, my legs were going to take me to him. Miles flew by, and I dipped onto the hidden access road that led into the heart of the city. The forest disappeared and became a blur of concrete.

Maybe I had gone insane. Maybe that was what love did to us. Made us do crazy, stupid things.

My legs were on the verge of giving out beneath me, and everything else felt like it was on fire. Still, I kept going.

I had to keep going. I wanted us to be together, like we were destined to be. *Truly* together. Bonded mates at each other's sides.

I collapsed in front of his apartment building, and slowly, on shaking legs, shifted back to my human form. I stood up, drenched in sweat and gasping for breath, and called up to his window.

. . .

"Mason! Mason!"

I picked up a rock and tossed it at the window. Then I fumbled into my pocket for my phone, but it was missing. In my haste, I'd left it at the house.

"Dammit," I muttered between breaths.

"Mr. Luna?"

I looked up at the window, and saw Mason's mother's face peering down at me.

"Ma'am," I said, still trying to catch my breath, my hands on my knees. "Is Mason here?"

"Mason is out at the store. Let me come open the door for you."

"Oh, Mrs. Arkentooth, you don't have to," I protested, but she was already gone from the window.

I waited down in the building's entrance, and a short while later she appeared to open the door.

. . .

"Thank you, Mrs. Arkentooth." I said.

"Please, call me Eliza. I think you need a towel," she said, looking up at me from her wheelchair. "Are you okay?"

I nodded. "I'm fine."

Up in the apartment, she got me a glass of water and a towel, and I wiped off my sweat-drenched face and sat down on the couch with a grateful groan.

"Your daughter's not here?" I asked.

"She's back in school," she replied with a smile. "Mr. Luna, I want to thank you for giving Mason work. It's been a great help to us."

"Oh, no, it's nothing," I managed, still trying to catch my breath.

"It's not nothing. You don't know how much you've helped us." She pushed her chair so that she was seated across from me.

"Are you *sure* you're alright? You look like you've just ran a marathon."

. . .

"Well… that's not so far from the truth. I ran here."

"Why would you do something like that?"

"It's… complicated." Looking at her now, I could see what Mason meant—it was obvious how limited her movements were. I felt terrible for making her come all the way down to open the door for me, but she seemed like the kind of woman who you couldn't say no to. In that sense, she reminded me of my own mother.

"Okay," she said, and took my glass. "I'll get you some more water."

"Oh, I can—"

"No, you sit down. You look like you're about to pass out. I can get you the water."

She pushed herself over to the kitchen and I stayed on the couch. A clock ticked softly on the wall. I stared at it, slowly going over what I'd done. A feeling of shame had begun to spread through me, like the pressure of deep water. I didn't want to have to decide between my family and Mason. It was ridiculous that I had to.

. . .

"He's always working so hard," Mrs. Arkentooth said from the kitchen. "I know it's so difficult for him. Mason has had to look after this family ever since his father passed. And my condition only made things worse. He's sacrificed so much for the family. I know he'd give everything for us, and that worries me. He needs to live his own life, too."

I felt a painful tightening around my heart. "I understand," I said. "Family is everything. I'd do anything for mine."

"Yes!" She came back into the living room and handed me the refilled glass of water. "Which is why I've been trying for so long to convince Mason of the importance of starting his own, of looking to the future. The boy needs to get out and meet someone. A mate becomes your family, after all."

"That's right," I said, stunned.

"Anyway, that's why I'm so thankful you've given him an opportunity to work, Mr. Luna. He'll always be reliable to you, I promise you."

She seemed worried, and I suddenly realized that she must've thought I'd come to deliver bad news.

"Mrs. Arkentooth—I mean, Eliza—please. Listen… You must think I'm here to speak to Mason about his work, but the truth is… Well, the truth is that there isn't any work."

. . .

"Oh," she said, looking flattened.

"No, no. What I mean is, Mason… He and I…"

At that moment, the lock to the front door turned. We both looked over as the door pushed open and Mason walked in, bags of groceries hanging from his arms.

"Mom, I'm back—"

The moment he saw me, he lost his grip on one of the bags and it fell to the floor, sending oranges and potatoes rolling across the floor. I stood up and strode over to him. I was unable to stop myself. I'd wanted to see him and hold him so badly that it all just came out. I wrapped my arms around him, pulling him tightly against my body. He stood there in stunned silence for a moment before lowering the other bag to the ground and slowly returning my embrace.

"What are you doing here, idiot?" he asked softly.

I took his face in my hands and kissed him.

"Oh," I heard Mrs. Arkentooth utter.

. . .

"I needed to see you," I whispered back to him. "No more secret meetings."

He raised an eyebrow at me, and Mrs. Arkentooth cleared her throat.

"Someone mind explaining what's going on?" she said.

"Sorry, Mom. I know it's out of nowhere but, well, Christophe and I are together." He gave me a questioning look.

"We're together," I said, taking his hand.

"This is all so sudden," she said, looking shocked. If she wasn't already sitting down, I would've been worried for her safety. "A surprise. A nice surprise. But so sudden."

"There's a lot to explain," Mason said. He gave me another look, and I knew exactly what it meant. *Let me do the talking*. I gave him a slight nod. Telling her exactly how we'd met would probably not be the wisest idea.

We sat down on the couch.

. . .

"Mom, have you ever heard of something called a fated mate mark?"

MASON

Christophe and I walked down the street to a nearby park, where we sat and watched a group of kids chase each other around in their wolf forms. I was still feeling a bit of shock that Christophe had showed up at the apartment and eager to find out why, especially after the talk we'd had the night before.

"What's going on, Christophe?" I asked. "No more secret meetings?"

"I told my parents about us," he said.

My stomach did a flip. "You did? What happened?"

. . .

A flame of excited expectation lit up inside me. If Christophe had come here and told Mom that we were together, then maybe, somehow...

He shook his head. "My parents don't understand what it is that we share."

I shrunk down, deflated. "I see."

"They don't understand what us finding each other *means*. The importance of it."

"No," I said. "I guess we can't expect them to. It's not something that would make sense to anyone, unless they felt it themselves. What does this mean for us?" I was afraid of what his answer would be.

"My parents can decide what will happen with the clan. Either Arthur takes over as second eldest, or maybe—"

I grabbed his arm. "Hold on. You're not saying you're planning on leaving your family?"

"If that's what I must do, then I'll do it. For the first time in my life today, I walked away from my parents' orders. They know I'm serious."

. . .

"You can't be."

"I am," he said, frowning. "Of course I am."

He said this, but I could see the conflict in his eyes. "I understand how important family is to you, Christophe. I could never expect that of you."

"Do you believe we're fated mates?" he asked.

"Yes," I said emphatically. "I don't think I've ever been so sure about anything. I think I've known it from the very beginning."

"Then that means you are my family. You and me and our children."

"Our children," I repeated. I felt tingly just saying it.

"Yes," he said. "And as long as we're together, that's what I care about. That's the future."

I held back tears. Christophe's willingness to sacrifice everything he cared about the most just for me had me overwhelmed. Everything about us had me overwhelmed, like it didn't feel real. I'd never been in love with someone until now, until him. That love made me want to run away with him forever, but it also made me pause. I smiled and took Christophe's hand. "I'm sorry," I said.

"Why?"

"Because it's my fault you're in this shitty position. If I'd just kept my mouth shut about meeting secretly... Look, I'd much rather continue to keep our relationship on the down low than force you to make such a fucked up decision."

"Oh, Mason. No, no. You were absolutely right. My mate should never be a secret. It was completely unfair and selfish of me to ask that of you."

"And it's unfair and selfish of me for you to be forced to give up something so important."

"What would you have me do, then?"

"Don't abandon your clan, Christophe. They need a man like you to guide them. The kind of man who gives people second chances, and sees the best in others."

He looked at me with those ruby eyes of his, the spark of flame in them glimmering with intensity. I could see him trying to think of a solution to this, and coming up empty. I could see the flickering sadness there, and that longing. That same look of longing I'd seen for the first time just over a week ago. Had we really only known each other for such a short time? There was something about Christophe that felt like I'd always known my entire life.

"If I have to be with you in secret, then I'll live with that."

When we came back to the apartment, Jennifer was home from school, and as we walked through the front door she jabbed a finger at me and shouted with a giant smile on her face, "I knew you had a thing for him!"

We made dinner, and after eating we sat in the living room and explained the situation to her and Mom. Christophe was obviously unhappy about the whole thing, and I was upset too, especially because I understood how painful it must've been for him to turn his back on his parents, but I knew he realized he had to go back. If I had to stay in the shadows, then I could deal with that—even if he was forced to openly take a highborn mate. We were fated mates. Nothing could ever change that.

Christophe stayed the night at our apartment, and after I was sure that Jennifer and Mom had gone to bed, I turned the light off and locked my bedroom door. Our lips met, and our hands reached and explored in the darkness, tracing and finding each other's excitement. I bit into my pillow, doing the best I could to muffle my cries as he thrust deep inside of me, our bodies heaving together, damp skin on skin as fingers intertwined and lips left desperate kisses. He didn't tell me he was going to come this time, but I could hear it in his breathing and feel it in the way his cock swelled and filled me up, leaving me full of his warmth.

This was how we would have to do things. Always in the dark, two worlds always separate.

But at least we were together.

"Christophe," I murmured into his ear as we lay in each other's arms. It was the first time we'd been in bed together, and the first time we'd ever go to sleep together.

"Mason."

"Trouble."

"Hm?"

"I think I just might've fallen in love with you."

I heard him exhale a soft laugh, and he squeezed his arms tighter around me. "You have no idea how badly I've fallen in love with you."

* * *

Over the following months, Christophe quietly arranged a new house for me, Mom, and Jennifer. He'd wanted to get me my own place, and Mom and Jennifer their own home in a highborn neighborhood, but I refused and insisted on a "modest" upgrade. Modest to him, but to me it was luxury and already made me feel uncomfortable. Getting to know Christophe had helped me come to terms with my bias against highborn wealth, but I knew that he was an exception. I doubted if I'd ever be able to get used to that world. With financials taken care of by Christophe, our family was able to finally be free from the Blood Gulch Clan, and became unofficially sponsored by the Crescent Moons. None of it was on paper, but Christophe made sure we were taken care of. Even though we no longer had to worry about money, I didn't feel good about relying on Christophe, and decided to enroll at a community academy to study leadership and law arts. Jennifer transferred into to a prestigious pre-academy, and excelled.

His parents knew about me, but still refused to officially acknowledge our relationship. It was difficult sometimes to feel like I was a secret, but Christophe did everything he could to make me feel comfortable and not like our relationship was something shameful. Even his brothers did their best to welcome me, though I could feel that they were skeptical. Christophe and I did our best to create some kind of normalcy in our relationship, despite the secrecy.

Two months after we'd moved into our new house, Christophe arranged for me to bring Mom up north to

Ursidcomb, the bear shifter town where his brother Vander and his mate Pell were living. The bears were extremely good healers, and Pell was apparently one of the best around.

I sat alone in the lobby of the clinic, staring up at a painting of a grizzly bear catching a salmon in a river. Ursidcomb was a small town surrounded by dense forest, and all the buildings were constructed of wood and smelled like fresh pine. It was probably the most soothing place I'd ever been to.

Mom was inside being examined. The front door opened, and I stood up when I recognized Vander.

"Good to meet you finally, Mason," Vander said, shaking my hand. His belly was swollen with child.

"You too, Vander," I replied, and gestured to his pregnant stomach. "Congratulations. How much longer do you have?"

He smiled. "Not much time, now. A month, at the most."

"That's great. I'm excited for you."

"Thanks," he said. "Are you and Christophe trying…?"

My face went hot. "Uh, umm…"

. . .

"None of my business," he said. "Sorry."

"No, it's alright. You know, we've never actually talked about it, but I don't think there's anything we really need to say. I know we both would love for it to happen. It's just difficult…"

He nodded. "I'm sorry you guys have to go through all that dog shit with my parents. It isn't fair. They're stubborn."

"I understand," I said. "It's not like Christophe and I met under the best circumstances. I can't expect them, or anyone, to understand what we have between us. I am who I am, and I did the things that I did. I've got to live with that."

"I don't know your background," Vander said. "But I think that highborn, lowborn, wolf, bear—all of that is dog shit. All that matters is who you are inside. Your quality. Christophe may be a stuck up dick—no offense—"

"He totally is."

We both laughed.

. . .

"But he also is the best judge of character that I know. So that's why I know you must be a good guy. It's a shame my parents refuse to get that. But that's fine, you know? I didn't think they'd approve of me being with Pell. They had to deal with it. Eventually, they'll have to face up to the fact that you and Christophe are together for good."

His words made me feel warm inside. "Thanks," I said.

The door to the examination room opened, and Pell pushed Mom out in her wheelchair. She wore a wide smile on her face, and I perked up.

"Well," Pell said. "We have some news. Ah, maybe Eliza, you'd like to tell Mason?"

"Yes, doctor. Mason, it's treatable," she said, beaming. "Doctor Darkclaw says I'll be able to walk again."

My mouth dropped open. I ran over to Mom and hugged her tightly. "That's amazing! Mom, I can't believe it."

"It'll take several months of treatment and therapy," Pell said. "But I believe it can be done here with us in Ursidcomb."

. . .

"That's so wonderful," was all I could say. I was overwhelmed. Mom hugged me as tightly as she could, and I could hear her crying softly.

"I'm sorry you've had to go through so much for me, Mason," she said.

"No, Mom. No. I'd do it all again in a heartbeat."

CHRISTOPHE

Mother, Father, Arthur, and I sat around the dining table for another mostly silent breakfast. Ever since Mason and I got together, almost every meal had been like this. Arthur was always the first to finish and excuse himself from the tense awkwardness, and I delivered terse updates to Father about work and affairs, but that was it. I was still too angry for anything else.

It was ridiculous that I was still even living in the Luna manor. I should've been living with my mate and working on starting my own family. I was no longer a bachelor, though my parents refused to acknowledge that.

"We received a challenge from the Arctic Falls Clan," I said flatly. "I had it addressed peacefully."

"Good work," Father grunted.

. . .

"Anything else?"

"Nothing."

I left the dining room. I had some free time, so I was going to go and visit Mason at his house. He had the place to himself during the day, now that his mother was receiving care up in Ursidcomb, and up until now it'd been shockingly difficult to find time when we could be alone in private together. Those moments were precious—just being able to do normal household things together, not to mention being able to make love. We still met often at my place in the forest—it was the best place for us to be alone—but doing it on top of a rock wasn't always the most comfortable. Sometimes we just wanted a bed.

Or couch.

Or chair.

Or bathtub.

I fetched my jacket from the coatroom when I heard Mother call my name.

. . .

"Christophe?"

I turned around. "Yes, Mother?"

"Going out?"

"I've business to take of," I said. I could've just told her that I was going to see Mason, but I preferred keeping both of my parents on a need-to-know basis about all of that, which essentially meant I never told them anything.

"Okay," she said. Her typically cold expression seemed softened. She straightened my jacket and picked a bit of fluff off my shoulder.

"What is it, Mother?"

"How's Mason?" she asked.

I frowned. She hardly ever asked about him. "Mason is fine. Still my mate, just as before."

"How are the treatments going for his mother?"

. . .

I sighed. The only reason she knew about that was because Father had made a big deal about the healing expenses.

"They're fine," I said. "And she'll continue to receive them until she's well again."

"I'm not challenging you, Christophe," she said. "I just want to know how everything is going."

"Why do you care?"

"I care because you're my son. And by extension… That makes Mason my son too. So I want to make sure everything is alright."

"It's fine," I said, trying to hide my shock. Mother had taken a mostly silent disapproving stance on the whole issue, and I thought she saw Mason as nothing more than a lowborn thief who had somehow corrupted me. I lowered my voice. "Where is this coming from? I know you don't approve of Mason."

"I'm still trying to understand this whole thing. I can't say I do approve, but it doesn't change the fact that he is your mate. And… Well, I never told you this, but I've always disagreed with your Father about the fated mate marks and his opinion about the Teller."

. . .

"You have?"

"Yes. You see, Christophe, I… also was born with a mark."

Now I couldn't hide it. My mouth dropped open. "What? You and Father are…?"

"Your father and I were mated to strengthen clan and family bonds, like your brother, Loch, was."

"You had an arranged marriage?"

"Somewhat. We'd known each other since we were young."

I processed this. "Father's paw doesn't match your mark," I said.

She shook her head. "For a long time, I was convinced that maybe there was someone out there who did. I eventually realized my fantasies weren't fair to your father, and nor would they be fair to my future children if I wasn't fully invested. So I forgot about it all. Let it go. And do you know what happened?"

"What?"

. . .

"The mark disappeared. And I moved on, and fell in love with your father. But I think that perhaps, it hurt him quite deeply."

"That's why he doesn't believe in them," I said, and Mother nodded.

"So, I believe what you and Mason share is special, despite him being lowborn. And I've been doing what I can to turn your father's mind about it."

"Hounds of Hell, Mother," I said softly. "I hope… we haven't hurt you and Father's marriage."

She smiled and squeezed my arm. "Like I said, I'm over all that now. If there had been someone out there who matched my mark, they're no longer my fated mate. Your father is. And I believe that entirely."

I nodded, and then after a brief hesitation, embraced Mother. We both were not used to hugging one another, and she returned the hug, stiffly at first, and then more warmly.

"Thank you, Mother. You have no idea how much this means to me. I hope Father can come to understand us the same as you do."

. . .

"Someday," she said.

I drove to Mason's house filled with an incredible lightness. I'd been unaware of the weight that'd been on my shoulders, and having Mother's support had relieved some of it. It'd also given me strength. Not that I'd had any doubt about our relationship at all, but Mother's story had reminded me just how special Mason and I were. One thing different, and we could've ended up missing each other. The scariest part was that I could've put Mason in jail or something worse, but the universe had been on our side and brought us together.

Mason answered the front door and pounced on me, wrapping his legs around my waist. I grabbed him and kissed him and carried him to the couch.

"Someone's feisty," I said.

"You're damn right," he grinned, pulling me down on top of him. He threw his arms around my neck and kissed me.

"I love you," I told him.

"I love you too. You seem happy."

I nodded. "I am. This day got off on the right paw, surprisingly."

. . .

"I can say the same thing."

"Is that right? Tell me."

"Mm. You go first."

"Alright."

I lay down on the couch and wrapped my arms around him, hugging him against my chest, and then told him what had happened back at the house. To my surprise, Mason's eyes started to water, and he hid his face in my armpit.

"What?" I asked. "What's the matter?"

"That just… It really makes me happy to hear," he said. "And it's perfect, Christophe. It's so perfect for what I learned today."

"What did you learn?"

He looked up at me, resting his chin on my chest. His eyes sparkled and his smile widened into a broad grin. "We're going to have a baby."

. . .

My jaw dropped. "Are you serious?"

"Of *course* I'm serious, stupid. You and I are going to be fathers. I'm pregnant, Christophe."

All I could do was laugh. I hugged him and kissed him and laughed.

"We're going to be fathers," I said in awe. "Hounds of Hell, Mason. This is amazing. This is fantastic. We're going to have a family. The next Lunas…"

"And with this news about your mom, maybe this means that things are going to change." The hope in Mason's voice brought me back down to earth.

We still were living this separate life. Mother had come around, but Father was still as stubborn as ever. I didn't want to raise a child like this. A child wouldn't understand. Not to mention, my child, assuming they were an alpha, would be the next in line to inherit the Crescent Moon Clan leadership.

I made the decision in my mind at that moment that no matter what, this child would not be raised as a secret. If Father didn't acknowledge us, then there would be no more argument. I would leave to be with my family.

* * *

That night, I met my parents in the smoking room with a newly steeled resolve. Just like the time I'd told them about Mason and I, I walked around the room and looked at the portraits and ancestral artifacts that lined the walls. This time, though, I wasn't nervous at all. The eyes of my ancestors no longer seemed to be glaring down at me with disapproval, but instead were looking at me with encouragement. With pride. I was a Luna. Mason was a Luna. Our child would be a Luna.

"Mother, Father, please have a seat," I said, as I sat down in one of the leather armchairs. "I have some wonderful news to give you both, and I hope you can share in my happiness and excitement."

Something in Mother's eyes flashed. Father was stone faced and folded his hands over his stomach. "Go on," he said.

"Mason is pregnant. I'm going to have a child."

"Christophe, that's fantastic!" Mother said.

Father exhaled a long breath.

"Basch? Are you not going to say anything to your son?"

. . .

"There isn't anything to say."

"Basch!"

I held up my hand. "That's fine. Father, this is no longer in your hands. You won't decide the fate of my child. Whether you decide to be a part of your grandchild's life is your decision. But my child will be raised as a Luna. And I will be with Mason. The clan can wait for my leadership once you've passed, or Arthur can take over as next in line, it doesn't matter to me. You've always told me that family comes first, so I'm going to be with my family, regardless."

Father looked away. As prepared as I was, it still hurt. Silently, I stood and left the smoking room.

Mother followed me. "Christophe," she said.

"I'm sorry, Mother. I've made up my mind this time. No turning back."

"I know. You do what you must. I told you I was working on him, and I'll continue to do so. When the baby comes, please don't forget about us."

I softened and took my mother's hand. "I won't," I said. "I'll always be in touch with you. I'm not shutting anyone out. I just need to be there for Mason from now on."

She nodded. "Continue your duties to the clan. Nothing will change. You're still to be the leader, I'll make sure of that."

I gave my mother a hug, and left. As I walked down the steps towards the car, a part of me wondered if today might be my last day ever living in the Luna manor.

Mason was alone at the house, and greeted me with a tight hug. No words needed to be said; he could read on my face that it hadn't gone well.

"Jennifer went to visit Mom up in Ursidcomb for the weekend," he told me. "So… you'll be moving in, then?"

"Hope you don't mind," I said, smiling.

"Hey. You paid for the place." He grinned. "You can do whatever you want. Are you hungry?"

"Starving."

He went into the kitchen, and I followed behind.

. . .

"I've got some leftovers in the fridge, I can—"

I grabbed his wrist and spun him around to face me. "No, I'm hungry for something else."

His eyes flashed, and a smile crept across his lips. I pushed him up against the fridge, pinning his wrists above him with one hand, and gently bit his neck. He moaned in my ear and squirmed against me, and as I kissed up his neck to his lips I dropped my free hand down and gripped his stiffening bulge. Then I flipped him around, releasing his arms so I could get his pants off. He pushed his ass out, grinding it eagerly against me. I was hard, and I pulled myself out and without any delay, pushed my cock up to his opening and entered him.

He cried out and pressed against me, taking me all the way inside. I grabbed his waist and slammed in deep, going all the way to the hilt. After fucking him like that, I pulled out, spun him around again, and picked him up. He straddled my hips and I carried him over and laid him down on the dining room table. He pulled his legs back to open himself up for me, and I grabbed my cock and thrust into him that way too. The table creaked loudly under our rhythm, and Mason's cock bounced with every push. I reached down and wrapped my fist around it and began to stroke him in time with my movements.

"Fuck!" he moaned, and I felt him tighten around me. "Just like that. Just like *that*. Ohhh shit!"

. . .

I could feel the spasms of his oncoming climax rocking around me like waves in the sea, pulling my own orgasm from me like the tide. Mason's cock flexed, and thick lines of come spurted across my hand. I came too, slowly rolling my hips and allowing his tightness to milk every last drop out of me. I withdrew from him, and then leaned down to kiss him.

There was a loud popping sound as all four of the table's legs snapped and gave out. The table crashed to the floor, and at the last minute, Mason threw his arms out and grabbed me as he wrapped his legs around my waist. I stood there with Mason attached to my front, the two of us staring at each other wide eyed. He looked back over his shoulder at the decimated table, and we both started to laugh.

Mason's mother was discharged from Pell's clinic a month later, shortly after Vander and Pell's little girl was born. Living together with Mason and his mother and sister was such a big, but welcome, change in my life. Coming from my home, it took a while for me to get used to the new dynamic. I couldn't help but be overly formal with Mrs. Arkentooth, despite her prodding and urging to be casual. She demanded that I call her by her first name, but that was just so far removed from how I was used to treating my elders, not to mention my mother-in-law.

Mason continued at his academy, but decided to put his studies on hold at five months into the pregnancy to rest and prepare. Pell had determined that we were going to have a little boy.

Contact with my parents had been limited, though Mother came to visit when she could. I held on to the hope that Father would eventually come around. A good sign was that he hadn't done anything to impede my continued work for the clan, nor had he restricted my access to the family and clan resources. Officially recognizing my son as heir to the Luna estate and to the Crescent Moon Clan was a different story, however. I had no idea what would happen after his birth, and when he came of age, but I was prepared to fight. Alpha, omega, or even beta, my son *would* be a full-fledged Luna.

It was the start of summer, nearly a year and a half after we'd first met, when we had our son.

At three in the morning, Pell delivered our boy, Kota Luna, into this world. As I sat at Mason's bedside and held my little boy in my arms, I was filled with the most overwhelming sense of awe. Mason and I had created him. He was my son, the physical proof of our love. The result of fate, of the universe bringing two souls together in perfect harmony.

"Hello, Kota," I whispered to him. I tickled his cheek, and he reached up with his tiny hand and grabbed my thumb. "Welcome to the family."

. . .

I passed him back to Mason and kissed my mate on his forehead. He smiled at me, and I could see how exhausted he was.

"You should sleep," I told him.

"Not yet," he replied. "I've been working my ass off to pop this little guy out, I want to spend some more time with him."

I laughed. "You'll have years to do that."

"It's still hard for me to believe," Mason said, cradling Kota in his arms. "We have a kid."

I stroked Mason's hair. "I know. It's amazing."

"I honestly could never have imagined my life turning out this way. Breaking into your house turned out to be the best decision I ever made in my life." He gave me a cheeky grin.

"It was fate," I said. "It is hard to imagine how vastly different my life would be as well, if I hadn't met you. Honestly, it hurts me to think about it. I'd be lost, probably for the rest of my life."

. . .

To my surprise, heavy tears started to roll down Mason's cheeks. Kota cooed and yawned, blowing a bubble from his mouth.

I wrapped my arm around his shoulder and hugged him to my chest. "Mason? What is it?"

He shook his head. "It's just what you said. Thinking about you being lost… being hurt… I can't stand it. Damn, since when did I get so emotional?"

I wiped the tears away from his cheeks and kissed him, and then kissed Kota on his forehead. "It only makes where we are now that much more special, and incredible. Everything was against us finding one another, right down to the end, but we still did. We still met, and we still fell in love. I'll never take what we have for granted, ever."

"I love you," he said. When he smiled, a few more silvery tears streaked down his cheeks.

MASON

~~~~

I should've been more nervous about meeting Christophe's parents than I was, but I was too preoccupied with making sure that Kota was comfortable to think about anything else. I sat on the couch and cradled him in my arms as I murmured baby talk to him and tickled his chin. Mom had taken Jennifer and her school friends out to go swimming, so we had the house to ourselves.

Christophe was the most nervous I'd ever seen him. He kept a serious face and insisted he was fine, but he kept pacing around the room, occasionally sitting in a chair only to move to the couch, and then back to another chair again.

"What, are you testing all the furniture out?" I said. "Take it easy, huh?"

. . .

He nodded, and sat back on the couch. "Sorry."

"It'll be fine," I said. "No matter what happens. We'll be fine."

He answered with a distracted smile, and then chewed on a fingernail.

I went over and sat next to him. "Hold Kota?"

"Yeah." He took Kota from me and bounced him gently. Kota gurgled and reached out towards his dad's face. "Hello," Christophe said. "Ready to meet Grandmother and Grandfather?"

Kota burped and giggled. Christophe laughed and kissed him on the head, and Kota reached up and patted his cheek.

The doorbell rang. Christophe straightened. "I'll get it," I said.

"No, I should greet them first," he said. He passed Kota back to me, straightened his shirt, and went to the door and opened it. "Hi, Mother. Hi, Father," Christophe said. "Welcome. Please come in."

Now I was nervous.

. . .

Mrs. Luna gave Christophe a hug, and then came over to me. "Congratulations, Mason," she said, and I was surprised when she moved in to kiss me on the cheek. Her eyes turned down to the little bundle I cradled in my arms, and widened with delight. "And this must be Kota."

"Would you like to hold him, Stella?" I asked, and passed Kota to her. "Look, sweetheart. It's Grandmother."

Kota looked up with wide eyes, and Mrs. Luna beamed down at him. "I'm proud of you both," she said. "You've done well."

"Father," Christophe said, and after a moment of hesitation, extended his hand. Mr. Luna took it and shook it. Mrs. Luna and I stared on, tensely.

"Christophe. You've been well?"

"Yes, Father. I have. Would you like to meet your grandson?"

Mrs. Luna walked over to him with Kota, and as Mr. Luna's gaze turned down to rest on his grandson's tiny face, I saw his expression change.

"Oh," he said softly.

. . .

"Take him," Mrs. Luna said. "Hold Kota."

Mr. Luna took him into his arms, and a smile slowly spread over his lips. "He reminds me of you, when you were a baby," he said. "The same eyes. He's going to be strong, I can tell."

Christophe nodded, and with some hesitation, reached out and put his hand on his dad's back. "I think so too," he said. "I can feel it."

"You're the future of our family, little one," Mr. Luna said to Kota. "I hope you're up for the job."

I could see the relief shimmering in Christophe's eyes.

"How precious," Mrs. Luna said. "Look, he's laughing."

Kota giggled and reached up towards Mr. Luna.

"He's happy to meet his grandfather," I said.

Mr. Luna passed Kota to Christophe, and came over to me. I straightened up and offered my hand. "Sir," I said.

. . .

I'd never once before cared to give respect to anyone who hadn't earned it from me—especially not someone highborn—but things had changed. I could never be highborn myself, even as Christophe's mate. Being highborn was more than just money, it was a lifetime of upbringing that I didn't have. But as someone who now lived on the edge of both worlds, I was going to do my best to learn, to be an ambassador. And that started here.

Mr. Luna looked me up and down with an intense and penetrating gaze, as if he were looking right at my very character. I stared back firmly, resolved. I was no longer the same man who'd once tried to steal from his home.

He reached out and took my hand. His grip was firm. He didn't say anything to me, just shook my hand, but I was fine with that. I could feel receptiveness in his greeting, an openness to see my worth. And I was ready to prove myself, to show that I was worthy of being a part of this family.

Christophe came over to me, and I slipped my arm around his waist and gave him a kiss. Kota cooed and giggled, and I smiled down at him and kissed him on his tiny hands.

Christophe had told me that everyone had a destiny, and I believed that now. Fate had brought us together, and now we'd move forward together as one. This was the beginning of our lives together, the beginning of our new family.

. . .

The beginning of a new destiny.

EPILOGUE - CHRISTOPHE

I watched Kota play with his puzzle, his eyes focused intensely on the little cube shaped device that his Aunt Jennifer had given him. At five years old, Kota was a little smaller than his classmates, even for an omega, but where he lacked in size he made up in spunk and brains. He was far beyond his peers when it came to academics.

I looked out the window, watching as the passing skyscrapers of downtown Wolfheart thinned out. As we moved closer to Old Wolfheart the architecture changed, almost like we were stepping back in time, and I could see enormous stone temples where the all the ancient rites were performed. I settled back into the chair, and I felt Mason take my hand. I looked over at him and smiled. Kota laughed and held the puzzle up to us.

"Dad, Papa, I finished it!"

. . .

"Good work, Kota!" Mason said. "That was a hard one, wasn't it?"

"Not too hard."

The car turned off the private access road, and the temple grew even closer. Ever since Father had passed the clan leadership to me two years ago, the number of my visits to the temple had grown tremendously since I was required to be present for various ceremonies. Today, we were here for Kota, to hear the Teller's rites.

A year after I'd assumed leadership of the Crescent Moons, Mason had graduated from his academy, and this year he'd started an organization for lowborn neighborhoods to monitor and assist those who had been taken advantage of by predatory clans like the Blood Gulch. Jennifer had graduated pre-academy and was two years into her program at the Dawn Academy's School for Shift Technology. She was one of the school's few lowborn students, which had resulted in some unfair treatment from instructors and even a few physical fights with other students—all of which she'd won. I'd had to step in a few times on her behalf, but it was clear from her marks that she belonged there as much as anyone else. And with the advanced healing techniques of the bears, Mrs. Arkentooth had fully recovered, save for some minor joint stiffness in the mornings. Last year, she decided to do shift marathon competitions, where she'd run for miles in wolf form around the city.

. . .

The car pulled into the temple's lot, and Stephen rolled down the divider window. "Here, sir," he said.

"Thank you, Stephen."

He opened the door for us, and I unbuckled my son from his car seat. He took Mason's and my hand, and the three of us walked towards the temple's gigantic door. Kota craned his neck to look up at the huge stone wolves that sat on either side of the entrance, his mouth agape in awe.

Inside, the air was hazy with smoke, and I was greeted by that familiar smell of pine incense and candle wax. I felt Kota's little hand squeeze mine.

"What's the Teller going to do, Dad?" he asked. "What's he going to say?"

"He's going to look into your future."

"The future?"

I crouched down and squeezed his shoulder. "Are you scared?"

. . .

He shook his head, but I could see that he was. "What did he tell you, Dad?"

I smiled at him. "He told me about you."

Kota's eyes sparkled, and he broke into a grin.

"Ready?" Mason asked.

"Yeah," Kota said.

We walked together, hand in hand, towards the shroud of smoke that held the mystery of the future.

Want more of Christophe and Mason?
Download a special FREE bonus chapter, *The Date*! Keep turning till the very end of the book for the download link.

And if you enjoyed *Marked to the Omega*, **please consider leaving a rating or review**. All positive encouragement is a great help to authors! You can easily access the product page by scanning the QR code with your phone.

KEEP IN TOUCH WITH ASHE

Stay updated with sales and new releases by subscribing to Ashe Moon's personal newsletter. Scan the QR code below with your phone camera!

* * *

If you're looking for something a little more personal you can also join my private Facebook group, **Ashe Moon's Ashetronauts**!

My group is a safe space to chat with me and other readers, and where I also do special exclusive giveaways and announcements. Hope to see you there!

NEXT IN THE SERIES...

Alpha Arthur Luna has sworn off all men.

Thirteen years ago, his best friend was forced to be married off to another alpha, even though the two of them were in love. Determined not to have his heart broken again, Arthur has no plans to settle down... Until he discovers that Perry is back in town.

Perry Houndfang curses his arranged marriage. Thirteen

years ago, he didn't just leave Wolfheart behind—he left the love of his life. With a cheating, scornful husband on his tail, and a three-year-old daughter to protect, Perry's back in Wolfheart to seek refuge... But he wasn't expecting to run into Arthur again.

As they rediscover each other, it becomes obvious that fate had meant for them to be together. But Perry is still bound to another. To reclaim his love, Arthur must defeat Perry's husband in a motorcycle challenge; a death-defying race between two wolf alphas: winner takes all.

Bound to the Omega is a "second chance" story full of steamy romance, page turning action, and MPreg themes set in an exciting and vibrant new shifter world. It is the fourth and final book in the Luna Brothers Series, but is written so that it can be enjoyed on its own.

Loch's Story - Wed to the Omega
Vander's Story - Doctor to the Omega
Arthur's Story - Bound to the Omega

Also From Ashe Moon

Looking for something similar to the Luna Brothers? Check out The Dragon Firefighters series!

"A surprising adventure and decisions affect more than one life and the town. Great story. **Absolutely wonderful characters.***"*

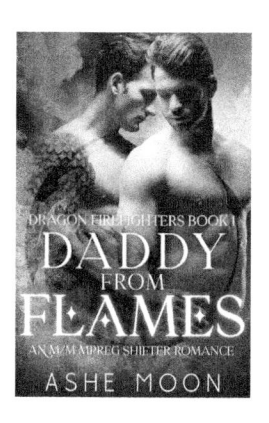

Pregnant and without an alpha, human omega Grayson must rely on his tenacity to provide for his unborn daughter. But when a fire claims his home and everything he's struggled to work for, rescue comes in an unexpected form: the alpha dragon Altair and his flight of firefighters who reluctantly take Grayson into their custody.

Altair's resentment of humanity is matched by a conflicting sense of duty to protect the town they share and all who call it home, human or dragon. He and his flight brothers have never had to deal with an omega before—let alone a human—and now they have one living under their roof! Everything Altair thought he knew about humans, omegas, and mates is called into question—and with Grayson's baby on the way, he's about to find out what it's like to be a daddy.

Daddy From Flames is the first book in the Dragon Firefighters mpreg series. This book features dragon shifters, a human omega, firefighters, an industrial fantasy setting, pregnancy/birth, new dads, a cat, love healing wounds, action, fun, light drama, and, as always, a happily ever after.

Scan the QR code with your phone camera to see the entire series!

Scan the QR code to sign up for my mailing list and receive *"The Date"*, the **FREE bonus chapter** to *Marked to the Omega*!

FREE BONUS CHAPTER

First Edition Cover

Copyright © 2017 by Ashe Moon

2023 - 2nd Edition

All rights reserved. No part of this publication may be reproduced, distributed, or transmitted in any form or by any means, including photocopying, recording, or other electronic or mechanical methods, without the prior written permission of the publisher, except in the case of brief quotations embodied in critical reviews and certain other noncommercial uses permitted by copyright law.